CW00858591

SURIAX

AMANDA YOUNG
RAYMOND YOUNG JR.

To RA McLain, a loving father and a generous, honest man. You will be missed.

CHAPTER ONE

KERN WATCHED THE BLOOD RUN DOWN HIS HAND AND ARM. THE cool blade glistened red in his hand. Those spots unmarred by blood were a clean, bright silver, making apparent to any who cared to look how well he cared for his weapons. With a sigh he pulled out a cloth and began wiping the blade clean. The body of the man he had just been speaking with lay lifeless at his feet.

"We need a recorder," he heard the bartender call. All around, patrons of the café glanced over briefly in curiosity and then went back about their business. A few didn't even bother looking. The door to the back opened to reveal a young woman. A full elf, one of the first to be born here after the founding of Suriax two hundred years ago, she was the equivalent of a thirty year old human. Honey colored golden hair, a length only attainable due to her long lifespan, was pulled back in several twists and braids. Her lips were lightly painted, it was the only coloring she wore, and she was dressed in an apron with her hair slightly askew. Her cheeks were flushed from her work in the heat of the kitchen, but that was not her only job. She worked there part time to help her brother Bryce, the bartender and owner of the Arrow's Quill Tavern. Though Marcy normally made her pay through her work as a recorder, they

AMANDA YOUNG & RAYMOND YOUNG JR.

were moving into the busy season, and the tavern could use all the help they could get. Seeing him right away, she smiled and walked over.

"Kern," she chastised with a grin as she pulled out a notepad and pen. "That's the third one this week. You know if you really wanted to see me that bad you could just ask me out and save the clean-up fee."

He grinned back. "What can I say, Marce? You're the best recorder in town."

"Umm, hmmm. You just say that because I already know what to put for all your information." He shrugged. Shaking her head, Marcy began filling out the form, mumbling to herself as she went along. "Let's see, name is Kern Tygierrenon. Rank: Lieutenant First Class of Flame Guard. Race: half elf. City of birth: Suriax. Age: one hundred twenty five. There, now, name of the deceased?"

"Cornerbluff."

"And was the reason for killing by order of the crown, for money or personal?"

"Personal." She looked up sharply. He understood her surprise. In all the times she served as his recorder, he never killed anyone for personal reasons. About ninety percent were ordered by the queen or other high officials. Ten percent were merc jobs he would occasionally take on for some quick coin. Either way, it was always a job.

Looking back down, Marcy found her place and continued. "Do you need to retrieve any items from the body?"

"Yes."

"Okay, you may do so, now."

Careful to avoid the slowly growing puddle of blood, Kern searched through the many coat pockets until he found what he was looking for. Pulling out a locket on a chain he checked to make sure the painting inside was still intact. Satisfied, he resumed his seat, tucking the necklace into his own pocket. Marcy noted what was recovered and handed Kern the form to sign. Signing under his name, she dated and stamped the document before putting it away. "So, are you done for the night, or should I get the next form ready?"

"You never know. Maybe you should come out with me tonight just in case I find myself in need of your services again."

Marcy laughed and shook her head. "Don't forget to pay Bryce on the way out." Kern watched her return to the kitchen then gathered his things and paid Bryce the clean-up fee, throwing in a little tip out of professional courtesy.

"You don't have to do that," Bryce argued. "You're easy to clean up after, not like those mages. They always want to be dramatic and kill people with fireballs. I have to replace the curtains every other month, and then the whole place smells like smoke for at least a week. You're no problem at all."

"I appreciate that." Bryce was taller than a typical elf, almost as tall as a human. Since most of his customers were half elves and full elves, he towered over a high percentage of the clientele, especially when he stood behind the bar, since the floor was raised there. A little extra height could be effective in commanding a sense of authority. It helped him deal with some of his rowdier patrons. "You guys take it easy."

"Hey, wait a sec," Bryce called before Kern could leave. "Could you take this over to your uncle?" He pulled out a small box and handed it to Kern. "It's drander pot stew. I heard him reminiscing about it the other day and tracked down some drander meat."

"Thanks, I know it'll mean a lot to him." He turned the box around in his hands. The craftsmanship was not the usual wooden box. There was a series of magical runes carved into the lid, and he could not feel any warmth from the food inside. "What kind of box is this?"

Bryce grinned broadly. "Lynnalin made that for us. It's got some enchantments on it. It keeps the food just the right temperature until you're ready to eat. Then it returns here when it's empty. We're going to start a whole new delivery service with these. With the Summer Solstice Celebrations this week we should be able to do some really good business."

"Well, good luck with that. If you get any more drander meat let me know." It was a rare find, as the ruler of the land it came from wasn't fond of Suriax and refused to trade with them.

"Will do."

All around decorations were being put out. There was excitement in the air. Everyone looked forward to the yearly, week long Summer Solstice celebrations to commemorate the founding of Suriax. Normally driven by the desire to excel at everything they did, in part due to the encouragement and direction of Queen Maerishka, this was one occasion in the year when everyone took time off to enjoy the festivities. There would be feasts, music, dancing, drinking and indulgences of every kind. People would marry, others would be conceived and vendors would make a lot of money. Some doubled their entire yearly revenue in the weeks surrounding the festival. It was one of the few times when tourists actually dared to venture into the city. With theft and murder legal in Suriax (given a few restrictions and monitoring to avoid rampant serial killers on the loose) it was not exactly a prime vacation destination. Those outside the city had this misconception that there were murders on every street corner, people routinely stabbed for their coin purses, and there was a certain amount of that, just as there was in any city, but criminals quickly learned that if murder was legal, so too was revenge killing. In more civilized cities, a victim's family must prove guilt, go to court and sit through trials that may or may not find the defendant guilty. But in Suriax, if you knew someone killed your husband or brother you could go out and kill them yourself without fear of being arrested or executed for doing so. It led to more careful criminals who actually avoided killing whenever possible. Most killings these days were on order of the Queen and she rarely troubled herself with killing tourists (unless they were particularly annoying and took the last pastry at the bake shop before she could get it – but that had only happened once … that he knew of). In a lot of ways, Suriax was actually a safer place to live because of its controversial laws. The people policed themselves, and they were happier for it.

Kern made his way back through the city, past the racetrack and academies, to his small apartment just outside the walls surrounding the palace grounds. As a high ranking officer with the Flame Guard he could easily get a larger, more elaborate home, but his uncle Frex had lived here for over two hundred years, ever since before the founding of Suriax. He would be six hundred and eighty this year. Old, even for an elf, he didn't have many years left. Frex spent most of his days now reminiscing about the past and searching for company wherever he could find it.

"Uncle, I'm home."

"In the back," he called, his voice muffled. Kern made his way through the apartment. He heard several grunts and thuds coming from the den. His uncle stood on a small ladder in the closet, his body half hidden by coats and boxes. He grunted again, another box falling to join the growing pile at his feet.

"Uncle, what are you doing? You're going to hurt yourself." Kern rushed to the closet and helped his uncle down, careful to avoid the obstacles on the floor.

"I was looking for a scarf your mother made for me before she died. It was the green one with the blue on it."

"That's over here." Kern pulled the scarf from behind the chair. Frex grabbed it and held it close, tears gathering in his eyes.

Kern pushed back a swell of sadness at seeing his uncle so emotional. "Bryce asked me to bring you this."

Frex opened the box and looked up in surprise. "Drander pot stew? I haven't had this in a hundred years. Where did he find it?"

"Don't know, but he tracked it down for you."

The gratitude on his face warmed Kern's heart. Just the smell of the food brought more joy to the old man's face than he remembered seeing in years. He grabbed a spoon and drink and let Frex enjoy his meal, content to watch and wait. He still had one more surprise, but he wanted to let him thoroughly savor the food first. Frex finished eating and sat back with a satisfied sigh. Kern cleaned up. When he returned, the box was already gone, returned to Bryce. His uncle rested heavily in his chair, his eyed closed and his breathing slowed. Although he was old, he was not a frail man, at least not by elven standards. To the many half elves who inhabited Suriax and Aleria, even the stoutest elf could appear a little frail. But he did carry a weary air about him. He had witnessed many difficult times first hand in his almost seven hundred years. With nearly double the lifespan of a half elf and seven times that of a human, he was mostly alone now. Gently, Kern took his hand. Frex stirred and opened his eyes. "Uncle, I have something else I wanted to give you." Pulling out the locket, he put it in his hands. "I got it back for you. The man who attacked you and stole it is dead. He won't be hurting you again." He didn't go into detail of how the man died. Frex had never liked the idea of Kern joining the Guard, particularly because he didn't approve of killing, a throwback to his Alerian days, Kern supposed.

Frex opened the locket and stared down at the painting inside. It held the image of a young girl. The resemblance to both Kern and Frex was undeniable. She had the same dark black hair as Kern. Frex's was mostly silver, now, though it was once the same color. They all shared the same long nose, blue eyes and slight curve near the tip of their pointed elven ears. She was Kern's mother and Frex's only sister. Kern had very few memories of her. Frex had raised him from the time he was a baby. She visited, but it was always brief. She told him they would be together one day. This was just temporary. Then she died when he was in his thirties. She and Frex were very close and he took her death particularly hard. There were weeks he barely ate, and the sadness in his eyes never really went away.

Frex was silent for several minutes, his thumb tracing the lines of her face. Finally, he closed the locket and stood, walking to a cabinet across the room. Taking out a large leather-bound book, he returned to his seat. "There are things I need to tell you. I should have said something before now, but I honestly never thought it would matter, and I could not bring myself to talk about certain things. But time is running out for me, and you deserve to know who you are and where you came from."

"Uncle, what do you mean?" He could chalk the cryptic talk up to the ramblings of an old man, but for once, his uncle's eyes were completely clear and his entire demeanor was serious. Whatever he needed to say was obviously important to him.

Opening the book, he revealed a map showing Aleria and Suriax as one single city.

"How much do you know about the history of Aleria?"

Kern thought back. "Not much. It was founded by King … Emerien. Then his son and grandchildren had a power struggle, and they split up the city, founding Suriax."

Frex cringed. "I have much to explain. Emerien was a kindhearted, benevolent ruler, and a good and loyal friend to those he cared for."

"You sound as though you knew him."

Frex nodded. "We grew up together. I stood beside him at his wedding."

Kern could not have been more shocked. Sure, he worked for the queen, but he hardly knew her. They only met on rare occasions when she needed to give her orders personally. She never remembered his name. To be friends with someone who founded a city was something else entirely.

"I still remember when he met Carol. She was a human, and he was a full elf. Back then such pairings were not that common. As long lived as we are, we elves have a tendency to look down on other races. Besides, if you live to be seven hundred years old, why would you want to choose a mate who will die in less than a hundred? But he loved Carol. Consulting with many wizards and clerics, he finally found a way to join his life force with hers. It cut his life in half, but it also extended her life by the same measure. Of course, since they were joined, were he to die, she would also fade away and die. His family was furious that he would shorten his life so dramatically for a human. He founded Aleria so they would have a place they could live in peace. Word of their love and sacrifice spread wide, attracting many half elves, humans and like-minded elves. Aleria became a safe haven for those previously outcast. Emerien's dedication to law and justice led to many prosperous, happy years for those who resided there. His rule extended north to encompass the mountain settlements and farming communities. Landowners practically begged to swear fealty to him to avoid harsh taxation and cruel treatment from other kingdoms. There was resistance at first. Kings do not typically want to lose a tax source, but Emerien's troops fought out of loyalty, not fear, and other kingdoms soon learned that it was not worth the trouble to resist him.

Eventually Emerien fell to old age. He was succeeded by his son, Veritan. Veritan was not kind or benevolent. He was a corrupt, vile man without an ounce of compassion in his entire heart." Frex took a deep breath and forced himself to calm down. "His rule was known as the time of Black Law. Many people were imprisoned for minor offenses. There were riots. People died. You were born during all this madness. Your mother asked me to hide you here, for your protection. Of course, that was before this became Suriax. At that time, this was mostly undeveloped forests and open land."

"Why didn't we return to Aleria once this became Suriax?" This was something he had often wondered. Frex never hid his dislike of Suriax and its laws, but he insisted they must remain there.

"I considered it, but anyone who may look for you would do so there. Here no one would think to find you."

"That is why you told me to lie about my age," Kern surmised, finally understanding.

Frex nodded. "The fewer people who know where you were from, the less likely anyone would be to ever put together the pieces."

"But why did we need to hide like that? Who was after me, and why couldn't Mom come with us?"

The pained look returned to his eyes. "Your mother wanted to come with us." Frex paused, uncertain in his next words. "You mentioned before the power struggle between Veritan and his children, but you did not say its real cause. Convinced things had gone too far after the death of their mother in one of the riots, his children took control of the city. More like their grandfather, they believed in the purity of the law. They blamed their father's perversion of the law for the chaos that led to her death."

"Their mom died in a riot? Sounds like what happened to my mother." It was odd to think he could have something in common with kings and queens.

Frex looked away, silently turning several pages. Once he found the page he was looking for, he handed the book to Kern. "This is a portrait of the royal family shortly before King Emerien's death."

Kern looked at the picture. The king was obviously old but he looked happy, and his authority was easy to see, even in a painting. He draped an arm affectionately around a human woman who looked equally happy. Standing in front of them was their son, Veritan. He was dressed in a buttoned up coat with a collar that reached to his chin, his hair carefully styled to command respect and display strength. Beside him stood three children, two boys and a girl, and their mother. Kern felt his breath catch. The woman had midnight black hair, pearly white skin and eyes a crystal pure ice blue. A slight grin played at her lips, her chin tilted up defiantly. Her spirit called out to him. He knew her face. It was the same face in the locket, the face of his mother. Kern felt the book slip from his hands and fumbled to catch it, closing it in the process. After several deep breaths he looked up at his uncle. "How could you not tell me this sooner?"

"Your mother did not want you to be a part of that world. She wanted you to have a good life. Veritan was corrupted by his desire for power. Whatever good was once a part of him when they married became lost over time. He and your siblings often argued. There were times he tried to have them arrested, but their own understanding of the law protected them. They were ever vigilant to avoid any actions he could exploit, constantly finding loopholes for anything he may try. Your mother worried about introducing you to that world. She feared a life where you would constantly need to watch your step and justify every action. Or worse, she feared you may take after your father and learn his cruelty. Hiding her pregnancy as long as she could, she traveled here for the later months and for your birth, asking me to care for you when she returned to the city. She urged the triplets to leave with her, but they felt obligated to defend Aleria and set things right. Eventually, they did."

"Who was that man who stole your locket, then? All of this happened forever and a day ago. Why would anyone even care about me or who my parents were?"

"I remember Cornerbluff as a child who lived in the palace in Aleria. His father was a gnome cook in the kitchen. His mother was an elven handmaid for your mother. Their marriage would not have been ordinary in any other land, but under King Emerien, it was not looked down upon. Cornerbluff grew up in the palace. With his mother attending my sister, and the way servants tend to spread information like a disease, I am sure he heard the rumors of your mother's pregnancy. He saw us together in the marketplace and recognized me. Once he heard I was your uncle, he put together the pieces and figured out who you were."

"Even so, what did he have to gain from stealing the locket?"

"Think about it. How much do you think the queen would pay for knowledge of another potential heir to the throne? You are Veritan's son and are a good eighty years older than the queen. You also have ties to Aleria, and whatever anyone may have thought of Veritan or how much pride they may have to be citizens of Suriax, almost everyone old enough to remember Aleria has fond memories of my sister. She was a beloved princess during King Emerien's life and a beloved queen during Veritan's rule. Should you wish to challenge your half-sister, the crown could be yours."

Kern's head reeled. He was a Flame Guard, an assassin for the queen. Now he was told that he could be king. The choice was his. Though to be king would mean civil war, death, misery and who knew what else. The queen would not go quietly. And his uncle was right. She did not get where she was by letting threats to her leadership go unchecked. She killed her own parents and took over the rule of the kingdom when she was only fifty years old, a mere child for someone three quarters elf. You weren't even considered an adult until around a hundred years old. To maintain rule at such a young age was incredible. She was strong, determined and a born leader.

"What you're telling me is that my father's policies and cruelty led to my mother's death, my brothers and sister deposed our father, and my half-sister killed him. That's some family we've got there."

Frex nodded in understanding. "I know it's a lot to take in. I didn't mean to hit you with everything like this. I should have told you as soon as the locket was stolen. I wasn't thinking clearly. It brought back so many memories, of your mother, her death," his voice caught. "Losing her locket was like losing her all over again. But there is no time for that now. You must determine who, if anyone, knows of you and make plans to protect yourself should the queen learn of your existence."

Kern stood and stared out the window for several minutes. "You must leave the city," he said at last. "If I am in danger, then so are you, and so is anyone who knows the truth. The queen would consider you as much a threat as me, and she would not hesitate to have you killed to protect her throne."

"This is true, but where could I go? This is my home, and I am an old man."

"I'll think of something. For now, get some rest. I'll be back as soon as I can." He kissed his uncle on the top of his head and left.

"Five gold on the scrawny one."

"Fifteen silver on the big guy for drawing first blood."

"One gold someone breaks an arm."

Zanden pushed his way through the crowd of people yelling out bets for the two men about to fight. The room was large, but it looked small with so many people piled into it. The only open space was around the two fighters. This was one of the many small fighting halls that surrounded the coliseum. Suriaxians loved to fight. They also loved to gamble. That made pit fighting a very popular activity. Some fighters made a profession out of it, fighting in tournaments for prizes and prestige. Others only fought occasionally to make some quick coin, vent frustration and work off stress, or even just for fun. Most of those in attendance were locals, but there was a fair share of tourists today. They were here for Solstice and for the tournament.

The Tournament of Fire came around once a decade, the final event of the Summer Solstice. Other years, they held smaller tournaments and fights. Those off year matches were usually just for locals, but this year's tournament would draw competitors from all over the continent. Only the best fighters would participate. Lasting for three months, the weaker contenders were generally weeded out in the first month or so. Casualties occurred but weren't overly common, maybe one or two a week. Once a fighter gave up or was knocked unconscious he or she would lose the round. Killing your opponent was not necessary to win. The winner of the Tournament of Fire received thirty thousand gold pieces, a medal crafted by the finest dwarven craftsmen, encrusted with many gems, and all the respect and admiration one could ever ask for. Some even received appointments into the military based on their performance and skill. Many of the best Suriaxian generals were once Tournament of Fire contestants and winners. There were few other honors quite as high in Suriaxian society.

With so much at stake, there were more than a few people with something to prove and a penchant for violence. There would be more pit fights and proelignisium this week than in a whole month. A proelignis was, simply put, a fire battle. There were at least three fire battles taking place in this very room now. The tourists didn't even notice. A proelignis was not as flashy or loud as a pit fight, at least not when done right. It could actually refer to a variety of things, including standing over hot coals or placing a body part over an open flame. The winner was the one who could withstand the pain the longest. It was how Suriaxians often settled disputes or determined the recipient of rewards. As such, most adult Suriaxians had at least a few scars and had learned to never show any hint of pain unless they lost a limb or received a mortal wound. Anything else would heal.

Zanden paused for a moment to look around. A dwarven man dressed in an expensive cloak and sporting a nicely sized battle hammer hanging from his belt leaned over the table, counting out the bets. He was well known around the city as the man you went to for all fight related issues. His name was

Larn, and he stood out from the crowd. Although he was only a little shorter than most elves and half-elves, he was a good three times the width of everyone else in the room. A massive man, especially by elven standards, he could hold his own in a fight and occasionally proved that when bets went sour. Larn Vrock had been born in Suriax. He and his twin brother Rand were the only two dwarves to hold Suriaxian citizenship. Their father traveled to the city at its founding to help design the prize medal for the Tournament of Fire. Although he arrived with several other dwarves, he was the only one to stay. Larn took over his father's business interests in the tournaments and Rand helped establish the marenpaie hound races. Marenpaie were large, foxlike hounds bred for speed and toughness. The adolescents were used in daily life throughout the city and adults served as transportation and battle steeds. Unafraid and far from timid, they were well suited for combat. Hound races were held once a month, except during their breeding season in the early fall. The final race of every summer was second only to the Tournament of Fire in respect to its ability to draw in tourists. As in the pit fights, a fair amount of betting took place at the races. Hapless tourists were often taken in by quick witted Suriaxians. Having the benefit of knowing how all the earlier races of the season had gone, they had a decided edge in the betting and were eager to exploit it. Some tourists learned after one or two visits never to bet against a Suriaxian. Others never learned.

"What are you doing here?" Larn asked over the din of betters. "Shouldn't you be preparing for your tournament match?"

"That's why I'm here," Zanden said. "I want to fight."

Larn's face lit up. "Well, why didn't you say so?" He led Zanden to where the other fighters were warming up by sparring with each other in turn. "Which one would you like to fight first?"

Zanden judged their weaknesses almost instantly. There

were five men. Two were half elves. One was human. One was a dwarf, and the final was a full elf. His clothes gave him away as a desert elf. As he watched, he saw the dwarf favor his left shoulder. One of the half elves was unsteady when he went to kick. The human followed every forward jab with an uppercut. The full elf and the other half elf were the most difficult to read. A slight flinch whenever the elf shifted his weight to his right leg gave away a hidden injury, and the half elf extended himself too far forward when he punched. This was too easy. "All of them," he answered, dropping his cloak. Those around him erupted into furious cheering. The fighters looked at him with a mixture of admiration and trepidation.

"What do you say, gentleman?" Larn asked. "Do you think the five of you can take on Zanden?"

"I'm in," said the dwarf. Not to be outdone, the other men agreed. After a few minutes to allow for bets to be placed, they began.

The half elf with the overextended punch struck first. Zanden sidestepped and let the man's momentum carry him into the wall, with the help of a well-timed spin and kick to the back. The man fell to a heap on the ground. That left four.

The other men weren't as rash. They circled him slowly, waiting for an opening. Zanden turned so the fires were behind him. He watched the shadows of those fighters out of his field of vision, keeping his eyes on the other ones. The human in front of him looked to the side and gave a slight nod. A shadow moved. It was the other half elf. The human jabbed. He dodged the jab from the human and a kick from the half elf, grabbing his leg and swinging him into the human. The half-elf's face connected hard with the human's uppercut. Quick to exploit the distraction, the full elf dropped and tried to take out Zanden's legs. Meanwhile, the human recovered from his confusion and tried another punch. Zanden jumped over the elf's legs and did a mid-air round kick to the human, catching his face with the ball of his foot. He landed and brought his heel down on the elf's bad leg. He was knocked down a second later by a surprise overhand punch from the dwarf. Zanden rolled out of the way of another attack and jumped back up. He rushed forward and dropped low under the dwarf's blocking punch, striking up at dwarf's side, just under his bad arm. Catching the elf who was in the process of standing, with a kick to the chest, he sent him reeling into the prone human. They both grunted from the impact.

Then the fight was on between Zanden and the dwarf. Zanden bobbed and jabbed, blocked and kicked. He was careful to stay on the dwarf's bad side, throwing a three punch combo that should have ended the fight. The dwarf countered with two blocks and an uppercut from his bad arm. That sent Zanden to the floor. There was a collective gasp in the room. The dwarf rolled his shoulder and stretched his arm, pulling it back to the ready without a hint of pain. Zanden rubbed his jaw and stood. "You were faking," he said, impressed. The dwarf nodded. "Now that's more like it."

The two men began their fight anew, neither holding back. There were few things as dangerous as a skilled dwarven fighter. One who could move quickly was a triple threat of skill, speed and raw strength. Normally such a dwarf could make quick work of an elf, but Zanden had trained for over a hundred years to overcome such limitations. His build was sleek, but solid. He could take a hit, and he could deliver one. He watched the dwarf's new fighting style and noticed a brief opening whenever he did a cross punch, but getting around to exploit it would be tricky. The window was too short to get a hit in. He needed to distract his opponent and widen the window. Allowing himself to get hit on the next cross, he stumbled back a step and retaliated with a kick. He needed to make this look believable, so he threw in a frustrated grunt for good show. Zanden barely missed the next cross. The dwarf grinned with an excited gleam in his eyes. This was working. He thought he had Zanden's weakness. When he tried the cross punch a third time Zanden spun out of the way and threw a back kick up under the dwarf's extended arm, landing a blow square on his chest. Not giving him a moment to recover Zanden spun the other way and took him out with a strong forward punch to the head. The room cheered. Zanden accepted a towel to wipe the sweat from his face and neck. "Who's next?"

CHAPTER TWO

"YOUR MAJESTY, THE PREPARATIONS FOR THE SUMMER SOLSTICE celebrations are underway. All the foreign dignitaries expected for tomorrow's ball and banquet have arrived and are being taken care of." Svanteese made a notation on his scroll and rolled it up, putting it away. He was an unassuming man of medium stature. A full elf, and one of the few to make the transition from King Veritan's to Queen Maerishka's court, he was no stranger to royal gatherings and responsibilities. He had begun his royal service as a tutor. Maerishka spent many hours with him, learning languages, history and all the other things a monarch needed to know. When she took the throne, he was one of the few she actually trusted with the truth of why she did what she did. He helped fill her knowledge gaps and gave her invaluable advice in those early days. It was for that reason she kept him on as her personal advisor.

"Excellent. I've been told the southern plains have recently acquired a new ruler, King Alvexton. I should like to meet him." Maerishka didn't normally trouble herself overly much with socializing with the other rulers in the region. Three in particular were always noticeably absent, but she didn't have time to worry about her half siblings now. She left them alone, and they left her alone. Everyone was happy. Personally she believed they were secretly relieved when she killed their father. They blamed him for their mother's death, but none of them ever had the guts to do anything about it. Knowing them, they probably took it easy on him on purpose to avoid any possible conflict of interest in doling out his punishment. They looked down on Suriax for its lack of punishment for murder and would never condone killing out of revenge, but they respected Suriax's right as a sovereign country to have whatever laws they saw fit. As long as Suriaxians respected Alerian laws when visiting there, the three of them didn't say anything. But they never came to the Summer Solstice Royal Ball. That would mean honoring Venerith, the god whose teachings their father followed. That was something they would never do.

Shaking her head to clear away thoughts of family, Maerishka turned her mind back to those who would be attending the ball. Most notably was Brenalain, a middle aged elf lord from the western desert settlements. He was annoying, arrogant and always left sand wherever he went, but his land provided many highly sought after spices. He was known to cut off trade to anyone he didn't like. With his lands on the border between her kingdom and the Alerian kingdom, he tried to play them against each other but Aleria didn't play. They offered him a fair deal and told him to take it or leave it. Given the size of their kingdom, they had the leverage to back up their proposal. Unable to afford not to do business with them, Aleria was the only place he didn't constantly threaten to revoke trade from. In fact, the entire episode only made him more difficult to deal with. At the least slight, perceived or actual, he would stop all his shipments. Inviting him to the ball each year played to his ego and cemented their annual agreement. A week of cleaning sand out of every rug in the palace was a price worth paying to get their hands on those spices.

"Schedule my meeting with Alvexton after Sir Brenalain's meeting at the mid-week mark. I'm meeting with Brenalain that morning, so let's make Alvexton's meeting an early supper." She always scheduled her diplomatic meetings halfway through the celebration week. Most of her guests left with the tourists after the first few intensive days of the festival. Waiting until then to meet gave everyone a chance to enjoy themselves first and made any negotiations much easier. More importantly, it gave her time to partake in some of the Solstice activities as well.

"Your Majesty, you have the opening ceremonies and exhibition fights at the tournament," he reminded.

"Is that this year? I thought the tournament was next year. Oh, never mind. Invite him to join me in my private balcony at the stadium." With the tournament beginning just after nightfall, she had plenty of time to visit with the clerics before the opening ceremonies. Solstice was a busy time for her, but she tried to visit the temple at least once in the early part of the week. The latter part of the week was spent almost exclusively in the temple.

"Yes, Your Majesty. Your Majesty, there is one more thing."

"Go on," she prompted when Svanteese fell silent.

"A half gnome, half elf by the name of Cornerbluff was killed by a member of the Flame Guard."

Maerishka laughed. "That's hardly news. Someone probably hired the guard because the gnome cheated him at cards or something."

"The reason for the killing was listed as personal, and a locket was retrieved from the body."

"Okay, so he probably stole it. Why are you bringing this to me?" She tapped her foot impatiently.

"Cornerbluff requested an audience with you this morning.

That got her attention. "Go on."

"I did some research and found he was the son of a servant in your father's palace from his time in Aleria."

"Did he say what he wanted?"

"He said it had to do with another heir to the throne." Svanteese cringed and took a reflexive step back.

Outwardly she remained calm and composed, her eyes the only thing that changed. "Find out which guard killed him and bring that man to me. I'll be in the temple." It looked like she would be visiting the clerics a little earlier than she planned.

Kern looked in on his sleeping uncle before heading off to the temple headquarters for the Guard. Maybe he was worrying for nothing. He walked around the entire city and still didn't know what he should do. Chances were no one else even knew. So what if he had family he didn't know? He'd done fine without them all these years. But was that fair to Frex? His uncle had given up his entire life to protect him. Kern never really appreciated how much of a sacrifice that was until now. If not for him, Frex would be living in the palace in Aleria, surrounded by family who could care for him a lot better than a single nephew. He needed to be around people, not alone in some rundown apartment.

Footsteps rang down the hall. A woman rushed by, bumping into him without apology. His response died on his lips when he saw it was Queen Maerishka. He stopped dead in his tracks. She turned down the hall, and he heard the door to the altar room open and close. She was here to pray. That wasn't uncommon. She was a regular at the temple. Before today, he wouldn't have thought anything of seeing her here. Now … now her presence meant so much more. She was his half-sister, and she could very well become his executioner if she ever learned of that fact. It wouldn't be the first time she killed a family member. If anything happened to him, his uncle would be alone, and who was to say she would stop with him? If she had killed their father, she would have no qualms over killing his uncle. After all, they had a different mother, so Frex was not blood to her. As much as he wished he could forget everything he had learned and go back to the way things were, he couldn't hide from who he was. It was time to leave Suriax.

Kern poked his head in the back door of the tavern. This time of night, most of the regular patrons were home. Things were winding down, and the staff was beginning to clean up and get ready for the next day. It didn't take him long to find who he was looking for. "Hey, Marce, can we talk a minute?"

Marcy smiled instantly and put down her towel. "Sure." Joining him outside, she leaned casually against the building, looking at him expectantly. No doubt she thought he would finally ask her out. She hinted at it often enough. If only that were his reason for seeking her out tonight.

"I need you to look after my uncle for a while. I have some things I need to take care of, and I don't know how long I'll be. I don't want to leave him alone."

"Where are you going?"

"That's not important. Can you watch after him for me?"

"Of course, but …"

"Thanks, Marce." Kern kissed her quickly on the cheek and dashed off before she could ask any other questions. He didn't have any answers to give her. He didn't even know for sure where he was going. He needed to go to Aleria, but he had no idea what he would do when he arrived. He would just have to figure that out along the way.

"You're looking at this all wrong," Eirae looked across the table at his sister, Mirerien, and his brother, Pielere. Morning sunlight streamed in through the window. They normally didn't make any rulings this early in the day, but they had agreed to make a special exception this time. Everyone was on edge. With today the first day of the Suriaxian annual holiday, there would be many tourists and over-zealous participants bleeding over into Aleria. Alerians were distrustful of Suriaxians already. Every year, there was a spike in disputes, frustrations, and lawbreakers to deal with. The three of them had their work cut out for them. It was their job to maintain order in their kingdom. Of course there were other judges to handle smaller issues and day to day infractions, but Eirae and his siblings preferred to be hands on whenever possible. Many judges from their father's time were corrupt and gave verdicts based on bribes. They unseated all those judges and began anew, training a new generation of law keepers. Since those people had a great deal of power over the lives of their citizens, the triplets felt a great deal of responsibility for them. They reviewed every case personally and stepped in to reverse any verdicts that did not comply a hundred percent with the law. Their impartiality and dedication to the law earned them the name The Three Lawgivers. Eirae was known as the Punisher. As his name implied, he focused on the punishments given to lawbreakers. He believed it was the fear of punishment that kept order and gave the laws their strength. Pielere was called the Protector. He was the most like their grandfather, believing that laws existed to protect the citizens and should be fair and kind. He and Eirae often disagreed on the subtleties of the law with Pielere more likely to call for leniency in their punishments. Mirerien was the mediator between them. She did not feel the law existed to protect or punish anyone. Laws existed to maintain order. Either protection or punishment could achieve that goal at any given time. She was often referred to as the Keeper of Order. People from all over the continent sought out their advice and ruling in difficult cases, and they took their responsibilities very seriously.

"We can't excuse unsanctioned trade with Suriax," Eirae continued. "The Farnesay gnomes were very explicit. They only agreed to trade their drander meat with us because we assured them we would not trade it to Suriax. If they find out that merchant sold the meat to someone from Suriax, they will pull all their trade agreements with us. We are just as responsible as her for letting this happen."

"But if she didn't know he was from Suriax," Pielere argued.

"Exactly, if?"

"She didn't know," Mirerien said, speaking for the first time.

Eirae sighed. There was no arguing with Mirerien's ability to read people. If she said the merchant was telling the truth, it was true. "Be that as it may, if we let her get away with an unsanctioned sale others will follow. They will all want to claim they didn't know."

Pielere flipped through their papers. "She's only had her license a few months. Mistakes at this point are not to be unexpected."

"She didn't tax something the wrong amount, or miscount inventory. This violates treaties and trade laws. All merchants know the penalties for violating these laws are severe; instantaneous loss of their merchant license, fines and possible jail time."

Mirerien stood and looked out the window, not talking right away. Finally, she turned and looked at her brothers. "There is no need revoke her general merchant license. Her mistake was not made maliciously, and she is unlikely to purposefully repeat it. If she is unable to accurately monitor who her customers are and where her products are going, then we can take away her license to trade restricted items. That cuts into her potential profit, limiting her access to merchandise and forces her to face the economic consequences of her carelessness. We charge her a small fine to cover the paperwork fees and put her on a probationary period where we set her up to be monitored. If she doesn't break any other laws or restrictions during that time, we can revisit whether or not to reissue her full license."

"Agreed," Pielere nodded.

"Agreed," Eirae added. "Now, onto the next case."

———

Maerishka took a deep breath and held it, waiting for her attendant to pull the lacing tight on her dress. "Which ones do you like for the banquet?" her event coordinator asked, holding up two plates. One was white with a colorless imprint of the royal crest on the center. It was elegant, but no one would even notice the crest through the food. She pointed to the second plate, blue with black edges. The door opened and Svanteese entered, looking less than thrilled to be there. She dismissed everyone else, leaving the remainder of the banquet decisions for later. She had more important matters to attend to.

"What have you to report?"

"We know the identity of the guard who killed Cornerbluff, but we have been unable to locate him as of yet. His name is Kern Tygierrenon, and he lives in a small apartment with an elderly uncle, but no one has seen him enter or leave the residence all day. Nor has anyone seen him at the temple."

"Bring in the uncle. I want to know where he has gone."

"Ma'am, as I mentioned, he is very old."

"I'm sure there was a point in there somewhere." She stared him down, daring him to challenge her order. Svanteese was an excellent assistant, but he was a little too soft hearted at times for his own good. He would do well to toughen up and lose the sentimentality. But he didn't sugarcoat things. He told her the truth, regardless of the possible consequences to himself. His honesty and loyalty were the main reasons she kept him around.

"It is unlikely he would survive our usual interrogation methods. If he dies, we won't learn anything."

She grinned. She knew why he was really worried about killing the man. He was a softy when it came to the elderly and children, a throwback to his days in Aleria, she supposed. But he made his wishes relevant to her and gave her a reason she could accept. As long as he did that, she could allow him to keep his misguided beliefs and soft heart. "As long as you get the information, I don't care how you do it. Keep in mind that latitude will be gone if we have any reason to believe the uncle has information that could pose a threat to me. Are we clear?"

"Yes, Your Majesty." Bowing, he left her chamber, allowing everyone else to return.

Without missing a beat, the event planner pulled out a scroll. "For entertainment we have …"

Maerishka rolled her eyes, not even bothering to listen to her options. They wouldn't bring her anything inappropriate, so which one she chose didn't really matter. Randomly picking the remaining details, she got rid of everyone as quickly as possible. This was going to be a very long day.

Kern thanked the shopkeeper for his help and hoisted his bag of supplies onto his back. He could be gone some time, indefinitely if things went well, and he needed to prepare for whatever he may encounter. That meant food, new weapons and magical items and a few healing potions for good measure.

"Kern," a man in the black and blue uniform of the Flame Guard flagged him down. A human with sandy brown hair, Kern recognized him immediately. His name was Thomas. Most of the guards worked alone the majority of the time, but they had worked one job together a few months back. The two of them hit it off from the start, working well together. One of the few humans in the guard, and a quick learner able to keep up with elves who boasted a century or more of service under their belts, he was hard to forget. Taking a seat at an outdoor café, they ordered drinks. The man waited for the waitress to leave, then leaned forward, lowering his tone. "I wanted to give you a heads up. I heard one of the queen's assistants asking about you this morning. He wanted to know where you were. He didn't say much but it didn't sound like a regular summons for a job. It sounded serious."

Kern nodded, downing some of his drink. "That happened faster than I thought. He must have talked to someone after all. I must go." He stood. "Thank you for the warning."

Thomas followed after him, unwilling to let it go at that. "So you are in trouble? Tell me what is going on. Maybe I can help."

"No, I don't want to get you involved."

"Kern," he admonished. We are brothers. Let me help you."

Kern stopped. Members of the guard often referred to each other as brothers, but it affected him differently now, knowing he actually had brothers he never met. "There is one thing you can do. I need to leave the city, and I need someone to protect my uncle while I'm gone. I've already asked a friend to watch him, but given this news she may not be enough, and I don't want her to get hurt because of me either. If you could keep an eye on them, make sure they stay safe until I can get back, it would mean a lot to me."

"I swear I will keep them safe until your return."

"Thank you." Clasping arms, they bid each other farewell.

"Kern!" Marcy ran through the crowds, bumping into several people who couldn't have cared less. They were too busy drinking, dancing and rushing to see the parade to notice a single elven woman running by. She counted herself lucky she saw him in the midst of all this madness. After Kern left her last night, she looked around everywhere for him, without success. Just when she was about to give up and grab some lunch, she saw him talking with another guardsman. Three blocks later, she still couldn't seem to catch up to him. He was moving like a man on a mission, oblivious to all the chaos of the Solstice activities. Down one of the side streets the first of the many

Summer Solstice parades was about to begin. It was the largest and most popular, especially among tourists who tended to attend more of the early week activities. In a few days, most of the tourists would give way to the unbridled euphoria of what was for all intents and purposes a patriotic and religious holiday. They celebrated the founding of the city, but they also celebrated their patron god, Venerith. Known as the Corrupter by those outside Suriax, Venerith was the god whose teachings inspired Veritan in the creation of the city.

Stumbling, Marcy barely avoided colliding with a mid-air acrobat dangling from strips of blue and gold fabric, suspended from tree limbs. Mumbling an apology she knew went unheard, she finally caught sight of Kern again. So intent was she on her quarry, she didn't see the racing hound barreling toward her. Lucky for her, Kern did. Running at full speed, he pushed her out of the way. The hound ran past close enough for her to feel its tail whip around. Its handlers ran frantically after it, yelling in futility for him to stop. Her heart in her throat, she could feel her pulse pounding through her veins. Then she felt Kern's broad chest pressed against her body and her pulse was pounding for a different reason.

"Why did you follow me?" His voice was husky, his lips next to her ear. Given the loudness of the crowd, it was the only way to be heard without yelling.

"I was worried about you. The way you left, I wasn't sure if you planned on coming back." Kern looked down. "You don't plan on coming back, do you?"

"I don't know. The way things are going I don't know what is going to happen."

"What's going on? What aren't you telling me?"

Kern took a step back, letting his arms drop from around her. "It's complicated."

"Does it have anything to do with that man you killed yesterday? Is someone after you for it?"

"No, it's nothing like that. I mean this all kind of started with him, but there's no one out for retribution … that I know of." Great, one more thing he could worry about. Oh well, if someone wanted him dead for Cornerbluff's killing it would most likely have happened before now. The man had no living family, and from what Kern learned when tracking him down, most people weren't too fond of him. So, chances were, no one really minded his death. But he could be wrong. Nothing he could do about it now. He'd deal with that if the situation arose.

"So, what is going on?"

Kern looked around briefly at the crowd. No one appeared to be listening, but that didn't mean someone couldn't overhear their conversation and tell the wrong people. "Come with me." Taking her arm, Kern led them through the throngs of merry goers to a small park. Away from most of the shops and inns, there weren't many people on this side of town. Still, he felt a little nervous at the prospect of discussing his current situation aloud, as though speaking it would make it true, make it all real. Up until now, a part of him still felt it was all a dream he would soon wake up from. But were he to share his knowledge with someone else, that delusion would be lost to him. No more pretending. He would have to deal with the reality of who he was, never to return to his former self.

They sat in a small gazebo, Marcy quietly waiting for him to speak. "I'm not a hundred twenty five years old. I'm actually two hundred and thirty two."

"You are a three quarters elf?" she guessed from his ability to pass for much younger than his actual age.

"Yes." My father was a half elf, but my mother was a full elf.

"Why would you lie about such a thing?"

"I did so at my uncle's instruction, though I didn't understand why until last night. He was trying to protect me. There were people who would want me dead if they knew my identity. The man I killed last night stole a locket that held a portrait of my mother. If the wrong people saw it, my uncle and I could both be in danger. I need to talk to some people who may be able to help keep him safe. I just need you to keep an eye on him until I can get him out of here."

"Where are you going? If he is in danger, shouldn't you take him with you? What if someone comes after him while you're gone?"

"I'm going to Aleria. That's where he's from, where my family is from. Where I need to go ... it's going to be hard enough getting myself in. There's no way I could get us both in, and I don't know what to expect or what kind of reception we will receive. If things go badly there I don't want him caught in the middle of it. And I don't want him to get his hopes up or get his feelings hurt if things don't work out as I hope. I know I don't have a lot of time to play around with. I just pray it's enough."

"Why do I feel there is a lot you aren't telling me?"

He touched his hand to her face and smiled wistfully. "You are the only person I trust telling even this much to. Besides, if you knew any more it would put you at risk. If anything happens use this ring to contact me." He handed her a ring from his bag, closing her fingers around it. "It has a communication spell cast on it, part of a matching set. As long as I have the other one, I'll hear if you call me."

"Where did you get these? They must have cost a fortune."

"It's standard issue for the Guard. We use them to report back when we're on missions."

"But what good will they do if you're going to be in Aleria? If I do get into trouble, you won't be able to do anything about it."

Kern grinned and pulled out a scroll. "Teleportation spell." The Flame Guard had a fair access to spells and magical items. Their organization began many years before the establishment of Suriax as a group of assassins who were also devout worshipers of Venerith. Needless to say, once they learned of a place where killing was legal, founded on the teachings of Venerith, Suriax quickly became their base of operations.

Veritan employed the Guard so often he was assigned a high ranking member, Marianella Mareash, as his personal guard. The two married and bore a daughter, Maerishka, the current queen of Suriax. The relationship between the crown and the Flame Guard was cemented with their union. An official honor guard for the royal family, they also managed to maintain some independence to take on whatever jobs they wished, as long as it didn't interfere with their royal duties. Members routinely disappeared on jobs. They also had the freedom to refuse any assignment. It was never a good idea to send an assassin on a job he didn't want to be on. Nowadays they were divided into two groups, those in it for the job and those in it for their god. The Cleric Guard designed all the spells and magical items used by the rest of the group. Every member was completely decked out. Of course they didn't publicize that fact, or they would constantly need to defend themselves from every two copper thief wanting to make a silver. And those who didn't want to rob them would probably want to kill them out of fear for how powerful they were.

Marcy hugged Kern tightly. "Be safe."

"You, too."

They stood and went their separate ways, both having a job to do. Venerith willing, they would see each other again.

———

Marcy cleaned up the dishes and looked over her shoulder to the den. Frex was already dozing in his chair. He stirred at a knock to the door. She felt her heart skip. There weren't many people who could be knocking. She was so distracted with her own thoughts she didn't notice Frex was no longer in his chair until she heard him opening the door, letting in two Royal Guards.

"Where is Kern Tygierrenon?" one of them asked. The man

AMANDA YOUNG & RAYMOND YOUNG JR.

was the taller of the two, and from the insignia on his collar, she could tell he was the higher rank.

"He isn't here," Marcy answered, putting herself between Frex and the men.

"Who are you?" the shorter man asked.

"A friend," she tried to keep her voice calm. "He had a job outside Suriax. I'm just helping out while he's gone."

"Where exactly did he go?" the tall man asked again.

"I don't know," she answered semi-honestly. She knew he was in Aleria, but that was a large place. He could be anywhere in the city. "He couldn't discuss the details of the job." That was a plausible story. Flame Guardsmen were known for their ability to keep a secret. It was a necessity in their line of work.

"Okay, I believe you," the taller guard said. "Bring them with us."

"Wait, why?" She sidestepped the other man as he tried to grab her arm.

The officer turned back to her and smiled. "If he is out on a job, he will return, and when he comes looking for you both, it will lead him right to us. Problem solved."

She didn't know what to do. She had to protect Frex, but he wasn't safe either way. If she fought, he could get hurt. If they went quietly, they could be tortured. If she fought and didn't escape, they could be killed. Of course, that could happen no matter what she did. Her options weren't looking too good. The guard reached for her arm again and froze. His eyes widened briefly before closing. With a grunt, he fell to the floor, a pool of blood gathering around him. The taller guard turned, but he didn't even get his weapon pulled before falling lifelessly to the floor. Behind them stood a human male, dressed in blue and black. His sword was covered in their blood. He reached his hand out, his face changing from focused killer to kind friend in an instant. "I'm Thomas."

CHAPTER THREE

Maerishka looked around anxiously. The ball would begin soon, and Svanteese had not brought any word on the uncle or the missing guard. The heat from the day was ebbing, but the high humidity made the cooler temperature less than enjoyable. Her gown hugged her uncomfortably, but she did not adjust it. A queen did not adjust her garments in public.

"Her Royal Highness, Queen Maerishka," The announcer called.

"Long Live the Queen," rang out in the hall. She took to the steps and made her grand entrance, not even faltering when she caught sight of Svanteese from the corner of her eye. Of course he would choose now to appear. Between the customary introductions to the other distinguished guests and the several requests she had to dance, it would be at least an hour before she could slip away to talk to him in private.

Finally, taking advantage of a lag in conversation with Lord Brenalain to excuse herself, she ducked into a private chamber adjoining the hall and waited. Svanteese was quick to follow. He approached her with a look of trepidation, hesitant to speak. "Spit it out," she ordered. "You've had plenty of time to consider your wording."

Knowing her temperament was not about to improve, Svanteese spoke. "The uncle is gone and two guards are dead. Reports from neighbors place a young elven woman at the scene shortly before the guards went to the residence. From her description, she is most likely Marcy Kentalee, a recorder who had dealings with Kern Tygierrenon."

"Double the guard around the palace, but do it discretely. We don't want to alarm our guests. And do a sweep of all the homes. They must be hiding somewhere. Find them."

"Yes, Your Majesty." He bowed and exited quickly. Maerishka returned to the ball, but her heart wasn't in it. Every servant caught her eye. She watched every stranger for some hint of hostility. Anyone could be a threat. She had not felt this paranoid since she first assumed the throne. Of course the vast majority of those she suspected of treachery then were guilty, so you could not actually call her fears and suspicions paranoia.

"Your Highness," Alvexton waited for her to take his hand and led her to the dance floor. "I must say, so far I am very impressed by Suriax."

"I'm glad to hear it. We are honored to have you here." They settled into a comfortable dance, standing a little closer to each other than was customary. She did not complain.

"I must ask, isn't it difficult ruling over a land with such unusual laws?"

Maerishka grinned. "Quite the contrary. It actually makes my job much easier."

"Really?" Alvexton asked, intrigued.

She nodded. "As you know, sometimes as a ruler you must do things that the general public would consider questionable or immoral to protect your people and maintain order. Here, I can do what needs to be done without having to hide or justify my actions. Everything is strictly above board."

"So, you have no secrets from your people?"

Maerishka tried to maintain her smile. "I did not say that.

But everything I do is completely legal, so no one could ever use my actions to unseat me or challenge my rule."

"I see," he looked off in thought. "Well, Suriax is lucky to have you."

They maintained small talk after that, not leaving the dance floor until the music ended and the banquet began. He smiled warmly when he realized they were to be seated by one another. Unfortunately Brenalain was seated to her other side, so she found herself regaled by story after story from his homeland throughout the dinner. She and Alvexton did not speak again until the meal was over and all the other guests began filing out. "I had a lovely evening."

"As did I." At least the day wasn't a complete loss, she thought to herself. But the time for relaxation and enjoyment was over. She had matters to attend to. No one would take her throne. Kern Tygierrenon would pay.

Kern considered his options for getting into Aleria. Normally, there was no problem. Citizens traveled between the two cities all the time, but if he crossed at a gate he would need to give his name, and they may have guards posted, looking for him. Also, Aleria would be more discriminating on whom they let enter the city this week, to avoid rowdy tourists. Aleria and Suriax were separated by the Therion River. It was hundreds of feet wide with only two bridges crossing it. On either bank stood a wall, so even if he could manage to cross the river, he had to find a way through, over or under the wall to actually get into the city. The main bridge was found at the center, northern side of Suriax. It was well guarded and was the usual means of travel. The second bridge was located at the northwest side of the city, in an area known as Merchant's Square. That route was even trickier.

Merchant's Square was a common area of trade and

commerce that stretched into both cities. Aleria monitored and policed the northern half, while Suriax took the southern half. The bridge between the two halves was not as closely monitored. People often traveled back and forth between the stores for shopping and trade. But the square was surrounded by a heavy wall and gates. Both cities tried to keep the activities of the square confined to that area.

He could always take the long way and sneak out of Suriax through one of the large exterior walls, then enter Aleria through one of the main gates, but that would take time and draw a lot of questions as to why a Suriaxian wouldn't just come through one of the Suriax gates. Looked like he would need to get creative.

Laureen paid the fruit vendor and carried her basket away, slowly pulling out the note hidden under the apples. This was the only way to communicate without alerting anyone to her actual allegiance. She felt for the usual seal, but it was not there. This message was not from the queen. Confused, she read it. The note warned of a rouge flame guardsman being sought by Queen Maerishka. Word was he may be in Aleria. Details were sketchy, as usual for this method of communication. It was signed with a simple "F.G." Another guardsman sent the note, meaning it was sent out of professional courtesy to warn her of potential trouble in her current job. She considered the meaning. For the queen to search after a guardsman to the degree that would warrant sending this message, he must have some kind of information that was a threat. That meant there was a better than average chance he would bring the information to the Alerian monarchs to seek help or sanctuary. If he posed a threat to the crown, it was her duty to stop him. If he had simply got on the queen's bad side and wanted escape, she couldn't care less. As long as he didn't cross her or expose her Suriaxian origin, he could keep his life and his secrets. She tucked the note into a pocket and brought the food to the palace kitchen. Pretending to check the stew, she dropped the paper in the fire and watched it burn.

———

Kern crashed through the roof, landing on the floor of a small room. He had really thought that branch would hold. Closing his eyes, he took inventory of all his body parts. With the way his head was throbbing, and the loud music playing in the next room, it took some time. The beautiful bells melody of a music box filled the air. Then the song ended, and he was left in silence. A fast knock sounded at the door. Kern froze. "Coming." An elderly woman walked into the room and stopped, looking at Kern and up at the hole in the ceiling.

"Royal Guard," the man behind the door called.

Kern pleaded silently. Walking around the mess in the room, she made her way to the door, never taking her eyes off him until she cracked the door open. "Yes, can I help you?"

"We're looking for a man, half elf, who was seen around here."

"Oh, my, what is he wanted for?" She asked with all sincerity.

"He is wanted by the queen for questioning"

"Well, I haven't seen anything."

"Ma'am, your neighbors heard some strange noises coming from your apartment. If I could just …" he tried to push his way in, but she didn't budge.

"That was just me. I'm not as graceful as I used to be. Tripped on my rug coming into the living room and knocked over some things. Caused quite a mess, I'm afraid. If you'd like to help me clean …"

Her invitation had the desired effect. The guard mumbled a vague excuse and left. Kern waited until he couldn't hear anyone outside before moving. "Thank you for not telling him I was here."

The woman waved his thanks away. "What did you do to get the Royal Guard on your back? And how did you find yourself falling through my roof ... which you will be paying to repair, of course."

"Of course," he dusted his pants off. "I saw the guard and tried to bide my time hiding in the tree branches above your home. Misjudged the strength of one, and you know the rest."

She nodded. "There were a few branches hit by lightning in the last storm. You probably stepped on one of those. And why did you need to hide in the first place?"

"You're probably better off not knowing."

"Fair enough."

Kern cracked the front door and looked for any sign of the guard. Pulling a coin purse out of his bag, he handed it to the woman. "This should cover the repairs." He thought for a moment and considered his options. "You wouldn't happen to know a quiet way into Aleria?"

The old lady grinned. "That will be extra."

A few hours later, Kern was hiding in a carriage carrying fruit and goods, riding over the bridge to Aleria. Once they were through the second gate, the driver, the old lady's neighbor, lifted the blanket covered in produce and let him out. He chastised himself that he hadn't thought to check with a fruit vendor sooner. The Guard used them so often to courier messages discretely between the cities, such correspondences were known as "sending a cabbage." Of course he never knew they also transported people.

Kern looked around the city. He never took any jobs in Aleria, at his uncle's request, so this was a first for him. From the gate he could see the edge of a park. Both cities boasted parks at their center. With a large population of elves and half elves who favored being around nature, parks, homes and businesses built within trees and other plant life were common.

But from his limited view, he could see Aleria's park was easily four times that of Suriax's. Unable to help himself, he walked around there first. At the center of the park was a gazebo larger than most homes. It was decorated in flowers and ribbons. Chairs lined one side. Kern climbed a fairly large hill and looked around. You could see most of the city from there. The palace was north. To the east was a theater surrounded by inns and taverns. Whereas most people who visited Suriax came for the pit fighting or hound races, Aleria was known for its magnificent plays and music. Years of planning went into each production, and those who saw the plays talked about them endlessly for months afterwards. He heard they once recreated a battle at sea by flooding an inner level of the theater tree. The audience watched from seats nested among the branches. He always wanted to come here and view a show. Maybe he could bring his uncle to one later.

Kern looked back at the palace. It couldn't hurt to look around the city a little on his way there. He was very curious about this place that could have been his home. Sliding down the hill, he headed for the street.

———

Maerishka entered the temple and bowed respectfully. She began her study with the clerics at a young age. Her father insisted on it, convinced pushing his daughter to worship Venerith would cause the god to bestow blessings upon him. That was before her parents conspired to kill her. Few people knew the entire story as to why she had killed her parents. Veritan was a suspicious man. He grew to fear she would follow the example of her half siblings and have him overthrown. Her mother did not believe him at first, but he sowed the seeds of doubt and led her to seek a divination to learn if she would ever betray them. The answer was a simple "yes." Instantly, she made plans to have Maerishka murdered on her daily ride to the country. What she did not know was that a maid overheard her plans and warned Maerishka. Ironically, it was their plans to kill her that led to her betrayal. She had never considered it before, but as much as she loved her parents, self-preservation won out. So, she poisoned their drinks and took the throne at a mere fifty years of age. Her method of attaining the throne was enough to help her keep it at first. No one wanted to cross someone cold enough to kill her own parents for power. No one else needed to know it was really out of self-defense. To keep the throne, she had to become the conniving, calculating, power hungry woman they all believed her to be. It was exhausting, but she grew used to it. Now she would stop at nothing to keep her throne. Anything less was not an option.

Kneeling by the altar, she made her customary sacrifice and prayed for guidance and blessings. Her stomach churned. Who dare think they could take her throne? She made Suriax what it was today. She pushed everyone to innovate, to be their best. Every job was important. The farmers created more efficient means to grow and harvest food. The architects were challenged to design creative and impossible buildings able to withstand weather and push the envelope artistically. The magi were pushed to develop more powerful spells. Despite Suriax's reputation for its questionable laws, her people were respected for their skills and often sought after for jobs all across the continent. She would not allow anyone to take what she built away from her.

"My Lord, hear my prayers. I have served you faithfully and will continue to do so until my dying breath. I shaped this kingdom and all her citizens to honor you. Everything I do is to honor you. This city belongs to you and you alone. Take her and all Suriaxians. I ask only that I am allowed to lead them, to spread your glory. Use us, bless us, allow us… allow me the tools to succeed." She felt a burning in her belly and continued. "I am yours. Suriax is yours. Do with us what you will." She looked up at the statue of Venerith that sat behind the altar. It was older than the city, brought in with the Flame Guard when they moved to Suriax shortly after its founding. Impressive in size, even though it showed him seated, the statue measured over six foot in height and showed him holding a large scroll. It was said if one put his or her hand on the scroll and swore an oath or made a bargain with Venerith, it became a binding agreement and not something to be entered into lightly. Your name was forever etched into the stone in the language of the gods. There were only three other names there. She approached the statue and felt the pressure in the room grow heavy. The candle flames turned to blue, casting an eerie glow over the room. The burning inside her spread to her chest. Before she could change her mind, she slapped her hand onto the stone scroll. "I give you Suriax and all her citizens in exchange for the power to keep my throne." Her hand burned hot enough to make her scream, but she could not lift if from the stone. She watched in horror as blue flames rose from the scroll and ran up her arm, licking at the sides of her neck and face. She struggled to breathe. The room behind the statue disappeared into darkness, ethereal eyes staring at her from either side of the statue's head. A deep voice, soft, yet menacing echoed through the room, "Accepted." A white hot agony seared through her skin and body. In a flash, the flames pulled back into the statue, the shadows returned to normal. The eyes were gone. She could almost believe she had imagined the entire thing, but her arm was covered in dark flame shaped markings. The stone scroll flashed for an instant, fire carving her name into the stone. She realized belatedly her name was not written in any language she knew, yet she was able to read it. The other names were still a mystery to her. Holding her arm she stumbled from the room, wondering what she had just done.

———

"The coast is clear. Let's go." Thomas led Marcy and Frex through alleys and side streets, taking them to a patch of forest where they could travel unseen. The sun had long since disappeared behind the trees, leaving them in the dark without much warmth. Thankfully Thomas had a small lantern, but it didn't give off much light. Once they had made it a fair distance from the apartment, Thomas made camp. Marcy helped make Frex comfortable, waiting until he was asleep. Then she joined Thomas by the fire.

"So, you're in the Guard with Kern? I didn't think there were that many humans in the Guard."

"No, not many." He scratched the side of his face. "Come to think of it, I don't think I've met any others. But then, we don't exactly socialize that much with each other. We usually work alone."

"What made you join?"

He shrugged. "It's a job."

"There are plenty of jobs. Are you from Suriax?"

"No, I'm from a small village on a plateau in the mountains. When I was a boy, my village went through several difficult summers. There was no rain for months. All the crops began to fail. People were starving. Many picked up and left in search of food and opportunities. My father was stubborn. Our family had lived on that land for generations, and he didn't want to leave. When he died, I was left in charge of the family. I was young and not as experienced with farming as he was. Things quickly went from bad to worse. My younger sisters and mother became ill. Around that time, a strange elven man came through town. We didn't get many visitors, as you can imagine. His clothes were well kept and made of the finest materials. He was well fed and healthy. He stayed for a few weeks, and everyone commented how generous he was with his coin. He overpaid for his room, food and supplies. One day, I ran into him while picking up supplies. He helped me pay for extra food for my family. We got to talking, and I learned he had lived in the village a long time before. We were a human village, but apparently he was once friends with someone who lived in the town. They were long dead, as was everyone who knew him there, but he remembered his time in our village fondly and wanted to help out. I asked how he was able to afford such generosity. He told me he worked for the Flame Guard in Suriax. I had heard of the Guard before, but I thought they were all just a bunch of clerics sitting around praying and learning to fight. He told me about the mercenary branch, how some guardsmen were recruited specifically for jobs and spent considerably less time involved in worship and prayer. The more he talked, the more I realized I could be one of them and earn the money we needed to keep my family fed. He brought me back and I've been working here ever since. I keep what money I need for basic necessities and send back the rest to my family. Through working here, I made enough to pay for dowries for two of my sisters. My other sister and mother never go hungry, and there's even enough left over to help some of the other villagers from time to time. The droughts aren't usually a problem anymore, but years of poor crops and hardship took their toll. Many over-farmed the land that would produce to the point of worthlessness now. Many of the better farmers have died or moved on, and those who remain are more like me, men who worked on the farms but who don't really know enough to run them alone. I take back food and supplies when I can. The Guard has helped me do that."

"Do you ever plan to go back?" Given how much he cared for his home and his people, she could image how difficult it must be to live away from them.

"I want to, but I don't know if that will ever happen. Honestly I'd love to settle down, farm the land of my ancestors and raise a family of my own. But if staying here is the price I pay to keep even one person from starving, that's what I'll do."

"What if helping us jeopardizes that?"

Thomas didn't say anything, but from the expression on his

face, she could tell that thought had already occurred to him. Finally he threw another stick on the fire and dusted off his hands. "You should get some sleep. We can figure out where we're going from here in the morning."

Marcy awoke to the smell of freshly cooked meat. Thomas dished out food for each of them and put out the fire. Dew covered the ground. Sunlight glistened off the dew on Thomas' pack and rolled up sleeping mat. "How long have you been up?" she asked, stretching.

"I didn't go to sleep." He handed her a plate of food and took food and water over to Frex, gently waking him and helping him to sit.

Marcy ate in silence, feeling guilty for not realizing someone had to stay up and keep watch. She never even thought to offer to take turns. Instead she slept and left him to sit up alone all night. At least he didn't seem too much the worse for wear. It was too late now to worry about it. She would just have to make an effort to be more considerate from here on. He was sacrificing a lot to help them. The least she could do was stay up so he could get a few hours of sleep. "So, what's the plan?"

"I talked to Kern through our rings last night. He said we should make our way into Aleria. He found a merchant who may be receptive to help us given the proper financial incentive. The man won't be back in Suriax for a couple of days, though, so we have to bide our time until then. I know a few people with homes near the river. We may be able to hide out there while we wait. After breakfast, I'll hike out that way and see what I can work out." Thomas looked over at Frex and lowered his tone so only Marcy could hear. "When I get back, you can leave if you like. Right now, the only people who knew you were helping Kern are dead. If anyone else finds out, you may have to leave the city for good. Leave now, and you can go back to your life like nothing happened."

"I promised Kern I would watch after him."

Thomas busied himself packing the cooking supplies into his pack. "It was Kern's suggestion. He frees you from your promise."

Marcy felt strangely conflicted. If he freed her she should be able to walk away guilt free. She looked at Frex. She still felt responsible for him. If she left, who would take care of him when Thomas was busy keeping them safe? Who would be there to take a watch or be a second set of ears? And if she left she would probably never see Thomas again. For some reason she couldn't begin to understand, that thought bothered her almost as much as anything else. "I can't. I need to see this through."

"For Kern." He nodded his understanding, a hint of resignation in his voice.

Marcy felt the irrational urge to slap him. Here she was feeling bad for leaving him to handle all this on his own, and he had the nerve to sound disappointed that she was sticking around. "Well if you don't want me to stay …"

"What?" Thomas looked up confused. Even Frex looked up from his plate at her outburst. "No, I just … I figured … why exactly are you angry?"

If she had been in a better mood, she may have laughed at his confused expression. As it was, she couldn't stand to be around him anymore. "I'm going to freshen up." Grabbing her bag, she left.

———

"Stop holding back."

Mirerien pulled back her hammer and swung with all her strength. Collin easily blocked her blow by deflecting the energy down and out with his shield. Spinning, he swung his sword around, even with her arm. She sidestepped and used her momentum to bring the hammer back around and up. A few inches closer, and it would have hit him under the chin. "You are making it too easy," he complained. "I didn't even have to dodge that one."

"This is only training." She advanced her attack and pushed him back a few steps.

"You must train how you want to fight in an actual battle. If you hold back here, you may hesitate or hold back in a real fight. Your enemies will not hold back."

"Are you?" she shot back.

"Fair enough. So what do you say we both stop playing around and give this a good go?" They shared a grin and began fighting in earnest. The match raged until the midday sun was high in the sky. At some point, Mirerien became aware of an audience. Her nieces and nephews lined the edge of the sidewalk, watching and cheering when she landed a good blow. Exhausted and out of breath, they flew into a flurry of blows heightened with grace she thought long since spent. Breaking from a particularly complicated attack run, they looked at each other and nodded. Mirerien dropped her hammer through its loop, and Collin followed suit with his blade. The children yelled excitedly and ran up to congratulate her on her performance. Collin smiled and left.

"That was impressive," Pielere, commented. "I see your training is progressing nicely.

She nodded. "He is an excellent teacher. Thank you for recommending him."

"I am just glad to see you happy … with his training," he added pointedly.

Mirerien paused in unlacing her bracers and narrowed her eyes. "What is that supposed to mean?

"Not a thing." She raised an eyebrow. Pielere laughed.

Not expecting an answer, she returned to her bracers. "I do not see what is so funny."

"Yes, I know. That actually proves my point."

"You had a point?" a small grin played at the corner of her lips.

"That's more like it. My point was that it is good to see you enjoying yourself. You smiled more during that sparring match than I've seen you do in months, longer even."

"I smile," she said defensively. They began walking together back to the palace. The children were too caught up in a spontaneous game of tag to notice or care.

"Sister," Pielere said softly, "I love you, but you are not always the warmest person in the world. I know our work is important, but we must remain grounded in life or we forget why we do what we do or the real people our decisions impact. When you find something, or someone who can make you smile, hold on to that. It is not insignificant."

"Father, come play," a young boy ran up and grabbed Pielere's arm, pulling him toward the other children.

"I wish I could, but I have a meeting I must go to?"

"Go," Mirerien said, "I will take your meeting." Gratitude shone in his eyes. As she watched him play with his children, she thought he might be right.

It was strange being in Aleria. A part of him felt relaxed. There were no guards looking to kill him. No one here even knew who he was. It was odd to think this was his mother's home. The people seemed nice but somewhat subdued. A stark contrast to the festival going on just south of the river, things in Aleria were calm and rather boring.

Taking a detour off the main road, Kern looked for a place to eat. A small bakery caught his eye. The shop smelled of freshly cooked bread. It was inviting, bathed in sunlight and warm colors. There was only room for three tables, each with two chairs, but the place did not feel cramped. The decorations were simple, avoiding clutter. An elderly elven woman smiled from behind the counter. Showing amazing strength and stamina for her age, she beat and kneaded the dough in her hands, then pulled apart smaller pieces to cook. "Fresh bread?" She asked, pulling out a pan from the cooling rack.

"That sounds wonderful," Kern replied, handing her some coins. He broke off a piece of warm bread and took in a deep, satisfied breath. The woman put a bowl of butter by his plate and went back to her work. Kern ate slowly, taking seconds when his first loaf was gone, and watched the people come and go. Most stopped for a few minutes, exchanging a few words about their families as they picked up enough bread and other baked goods to last the day. A young elven boy came in through the back door and began helping the old woman. She tousled his hair affectionately and handed him some dough to knead. They worked in synchronized silence, each anticipating the other's movements and needs. "Could you take down the supplies for the next batch?" the woman asked.

"Sure, Grandmother," the boy answered. He pulled out a stepladder and grabbed a large bag of flour from the top shelf of a wooden cabinet. As small as the shop was, most of the storage was vertical.

The front door opened and the boy stopped, a look of dread and thinly veiled anger on his face. Four men, a mix of half elves and humans, came in, snickering, They grabbed food off the display shelves and ate without paying. The old woman turned her gaze down, her cheerful spirit gone. "There you are," one of the men said. "You're late."

"I'm helping my grandmother."

"Business must be very good if you can afford full rent." The woman's eyes shot open with panic.

"You rotten son of a …"

"Alnerand, no," The woman put a hand on the boy's arm to stop him from advancing on the intruders.

The door opened to reveal a young girl humming to herself

SURIAX

as she entered. One look at the men inside and she turned and left without a word. The leader of the group smiled. "Or we could just stay here until you are done."

"Just go," the old lady said.

"Grandmother …"

"I'll be fine. You can go."

The boy ripped off his apron and left with the men. The old lady went back to her work, stepping up on the ladder to reach her pans. Kern rushed to her side. "Let me." She smiled gratefully and indicated the items she still needed.

"Thank you. I'm sorry you had to see all that. I can see you aren't from around here." She looked pointedly at his clothes. "What brings you to Aleria?"

"Visiting family," he answered honestly. "Who were those men?" Kern took a seat at the counter and accepted a sweet roll and warm mead.

The woman wiped the sweat from her brow and got back to work on baking. "The main one is our landlord. Originally his father owned the apartments where we live, but when he died, his son took over. He forces every family to provide one member as free labor in his other businesses and for personal projects, or he dramatically increases the rent to the point where no one can pay it."

"Why don't you move?"

"I've lived there all my life. Besides, there is nowhere else I can afford to live. He owns many of the apartments in the city, and the apartments he doesn't own are much too expensive. His father was a good, kind man. He knew what we could afford and didn't charge any more. But none of us had any contracts in writing. On months where we could pay more, we would. On those months where money was tight, he would let the rent slide. He was an honorable man and we were all grateful for him. His son is nothing like him. Without a contract, he could charge whatever he wanted, and he does. None of us noticed it at first. He said he would keep our rent the same, but he started

49

to ask for free help on his projects. Of course none of us argued at first. We were accustomed to the give and take relationship we had before. It wasn't long before he began "asking" for help every day. Then he stopped asking. Anyone who said they couldn't work for him was immediately given a new lease to sign, one with a rent triple the current amount. But just listen to me go on and on. Can I get you anything else?"

The woman reminded him of Frex. He felt the strange urge to help her, but what could he do? If they were in Suriax he could offer to kill the man, but that was illegal here. He thanked her for her time and the food and left her a substantial tip. She and her grandson would have to figure out a solution to the problem on their own. Right now he needed to take care of his own problems.

"There is bread in the pantry."

"Thank you." Marcy went to retrieve the bread and started making dinner. Thomas' friends had a small, one bedroom home near the wall that bordered the Therion River. They were a young elf and human couple with two small children. The elven woman smiled and cut vegetables beside her, making small talk. She was very friendly, and Marcy wondered what Thomas told them about their situation. She would never want to put them at risk, but since no one knew Thomas was the one helping them, it was unlikely anyone would search out his acquaintances. A little girl came running into the kitchen and grabbed on to the woman's legs.

"Mamma, I'm hun'ry," the girl said.

She patted the girl's head and smiled affectionately. "Dinner will be done soon. Here, take some bread." The girl giggled and ran off with her prize. The woman laughed and turned back to the food.

"You have a beautiful family," Marcy commented, feeling slightly jealous. "Are you two bonded?"

"Yes, for almost ten years." She looked off dreamily.

"I've never understood doing that, giving up half your life for someone. I mean … it's a big decision, but I can see you two really care about each other." She hastened to add, afraid of insulting her host.

The woman laughed. "It's okay. I get that all the time. Before I met Bradley, I felt the same way. But when you find true love, you realize you would rather spend a few hundred years with him than seven hundred without him. Given the choice, I would make the same decision again."

"You have to catch the ball," Thomas called from outside. He and Bradley ran across the yard, throwing a small hollowed out gourd they were using as a ball. Running alongside them was Brad and Veronica's older boy, Max. He picked up the ball from the ground and looked at it for several moments before dropping it again. Brad went to grab it, but the boy kicked it through the man's legs before he could lay a hand on it. The sound of laughter filled the air. Marcy smiled.

"How long have you two been together?" Veronica asked.

"Hmm, what? Me and Thomas? Oh, we're not …"

"You aren't? I'm sorry, it's just that the way you look at each other, I assumed."

"We just met. We're helping out a mutual friend with his uncle. That's all."

"If you say so." Veronica scooped up the pieces of the vegetables she was cutting and put them in the stew pot.

"What do you mean by 'the way we look at each other?'" Marcy asked, unable to help herself.

"Honey, Thomas doesn't look at you like a stranger, and there was something in your eyes just now too. Besides, that awkward silence between you when you arrived speaks volumes. No one can make you quite as angry as someone you care for. You may have just met, but there is definitely something there."

"Hey, Max asked for some bread," Thomas leaned in the back door. His hair was disheveled from their play. Marcy felt her face flush and looked away. Veronica handed him the bread and they exchanged a few words, but Marcy wasn't listening. Thomas was handsome, and he did save her from the guards, but could she really have feelings for him? She chanced a glance up and saw him staring at her. He looked away quickly, mumbling something to Veronica and going back outside. They cooked in silence after that, Veronica allowing her to brood on her thoughts.

Marcy didn't say much throughout dinner. She was so distracted she didn't even notice when everyone went to bed. Sitting outside, looking up at the stars, she slowly realized the house was quiet and all the lamps were out. She thought she would go to bed herself, but several minutes later she hadn't moved. She listened to the distant hum of music from the ongoing festival. Bryce would probably be wondering where she was by now. She wished there was some way to contact him without putting him in danger. Her eyes grew heavy, and she found herself drifting off where she sat. Arms wrapped around her and she felt herself be lifted into the air. Turning into the embrace, she rested her palm against a broad chest. It rose and fell with deep, even breaths, his heart beating loudly under her ear. She relaxed into his arms, feeling slightly bereft when he laid her down on her bed. Opening her eyes, she saw Thomas walking quietly to the door. "Veronica thought we were a couple," she said softly.

Thomas stopped and looked back at her. "What did you tell her?"

"That we just met."

He acknowledged her response through the slight upturn of his face. "Good night, Marcy."

Kern stared up at the stars, the grass at his back. In the distance he could see the walls surrounding the palace. The palace tree towered above it. As with most buildings of importance in Suriax and Aleria, the palace was crafted with powerful magic and expert designs from the structure of a large tree. He could almost make out the upper levels, nestled among the tree limbs. He spent most of his day looking around, gently probing people for information about the palace and its security. Now he had to decide how to get in. That could wait until tomorrow, after a good night's sleep, he reasoned. Closing his eyes, he strained his ears to listen for the distant sounds of celebrations. Aleria was quiet, most everyone asleep. He heard a horse shuffle his feet in his stall at the stables down the road. A cricket chirped softly. He almost gave up hearing anything when the slow beat of a drum caught his ear. One … two … three … three beats. It was the ceremonial drum announcing the start of the third day of celebration.

And then he heard the flute. Kern opened his eyes and saw a wedding procession walking to the gazebo at the center of the park. They were led by the bride and groom, walking hand in hand. The man was an elf, the bride a human. This was a bonding wedding. It was traditional in elven society to hold the ceremony at midnight and follow it with a full day of celebrating. Midnight was the start of a new day. The couple joined, not when all was light and easy, but in the cold darkness of night. Together, they pledged to face the coming day and all the hopes and problems it may bring. In a bonding wedding they entered the ceremony site together with hands joined to signify their added level of commitment. They walked as equals, already joined in their hearts.

Kern watched the couple step up to the priest and recite their vows. Clerics stood to the side, working the bonding magic. A glow came over the bride and groom. Their features shifted subtly. It was more noticeable in the man, who aged many years in the span of a few seconds. They looked into each other's eyes and smiled, happier than anyone he ever saw.

Bonding weddings weren't as common in Suriax. Full elves and humans were mostly bred out, and few new ones chose to move to Suriax. While there was a lifespan difference between a quarter elf and a three quarter elf, it was not as substantial as that between a full elf and human. Besides, Suriaxians were less willing to sacrifice any of their life for another, even for love.

The couple shared a kiss, and their family and friends cheered. The once quiet night burst into song and dance. In an odd way, it reminded him of being home for the Solstice Celebrations. He watched them for some time. Their happiness was contagious. He longed to be a part of the celebration, to sing and dance without a care, to know that no matter what happened, he wasn't alone. Tomorrow he would meet his family, and he had no idea what to expect. That thought in the back of his mind, Kern went to sleep.

CHAPTER FOUR

THINGS WERE ODDLY RELAXED BETWEEN MARCY AND THOMAS THE next day. He wore a loose tunic, borrowed from Bradley. While he looked dashing, charming and dangerous in his Flame Guard jacket, the casual clothing seemed to fit him better. He was a natural with the children. They ran up to him, wanting to show him a rock or piece of string they decided was an ogre, and he played right along, pretending to be scared. They would laugh and run off, only to come back a short while later with a new imaginary monster. This was who he was, not some hired assassin or mercenary. She could easily picture him turning his back on Suriax and never regretting it. The funny thing was, while she watched him she could easily picture herself doing the same.

The adults sat around the dining room table for most of the morning. They drank tea and ate a late breakfast, talking about how Thomas and Bradley had met. As it turned out, Thomas knew Bradley from his village. They grew up together, getting into much mischief in their younger years. When Thomas decided to leave, they traveled to Suriax together. While Bradley never had any interest in the Guard, he decided he too could find a new start there.

Veronica tilted her head to the side, her keen elven ears hearing voices only her and Marcy seemed to notice. "Is someone outside?" she asked, interrupting a story of how Brad talked Thomas out of letting a practicing mage try to burn his hair shorter for a bet. Bradley shot up and went to check on the children.

Going to the window, Marcy felt her blood run cold. "It's the Royal Guard." She and Thomas looked at each other, wondering how they were found so quickly.

"Can I help you?" Bradley asked, putting a protective hand on Max's shoulder. Vivian hid behind his legs.

"We are looking for a half elf Flame Guardsman who goes by the name, Kern. He may be traveling with an older elven man and a young elf woman."

"I haven't seen anyone like that around here."

"I'll need to check the house to confirm that," the guard said.

Thomas reached for his sword at his waist, but Marcy stayed his hand. If they got into a fight here someone, possibly one of the children, could get hurt. "I have an idea." Running to her bag, she pulled out a book with several scrolls loose inside. She flipped through the scrolls quickly, looking for the one that could help. "Ah, ha," she said triumphantly. Putting the book down, she ran over to Frex and took his hand. "Apelai Chamealton," she said. The scroll disappeared in her hand, dissolving into a glowing mist that surrounded them. When the mist was gone, Frex and Marcy had the appearance of humans. Before anyone could say anything, the front door opened. Bradley was the first to enter. He faltered a half step at seeing them, but quickly recovered. Marcy could see the look of relief on his face.

The guard looked around the room and then down at a paper in his hand. "It says here there are only four people living at this residence."

"That is correct," Bradley said. "Some of my family is visiting for the Solstice Festival."

The guard nodded and proceeded to check the rest of the house. He looked in every closet and cabinet, and he even pulled back the curtains. After checking the rest of the house, he came back in the front, looking around again for anything out of place. Marcy looked over at Thomas and felt her heart catch. Directly behind him, on the arm of the chair, was his Flame Guard jacket. One look at that jacket would give them away. If he found out any of them were with the Guard he would know they had lied about their identities, and he would not be inclined to look the other way. The Royal Guard hated the Flame Guard. They were constantly competing for the crown's attention. Technically the Royal Guard was the Queen's personal guard, but she used the Flame Guard often enough that a fair amount of jealousy developed. Marcy caught Thomas' eyes and looked over at the jacket. His own eyes widened as soon as he saw it. Stretching casually, he knocked the jacket to the floor and kicked it under the chair. The guard turned at the movement, but Thomas covered by sitting on the arm of the chair with a sigh. Apparently satisfied, the guard bid them a good day and left.

Marcy released the breath she was holding and let go of Frex's hand. The illusion melted away, restoring their normal faces.

"How did you do that?" Veronica asked.

"It was a change appearance scroll my friend Lynnalin gave me. She makes magical items for my brother's tavern all the time and threw it in as a gift."

"Do you have any other ones?" Thomas asked hopefully.

"Unfortunately, no, that was the only one."

Thomas looked off thoughtfully. "How could they have found us so fast?"

"I don't think they did." Marcy answered. "They didn't ask about you. I don't think they know about you, yet. It sounded like they were checking everyone."

"What did Kern get himself involved with?" Thomas asked

in wonder. It was no small feat to get that kind of attention from the Crown, especially during the festival.

"He said it had something to do with his parents, but he didn't tell me who they were."

Both of them looked at Frex expectantly. Looking uncertain, he shifted in his seat. "I suppose you should know. Kern is the son of Crystillia and Veritan. He is the half-brother to Queen Maerishka."

The shock in the room was palpable. "No wonder they're looking everywhere. If anyone found out there was another heir to the throne ..." Thomas let his words trail off. Everyone knew what would happen. There would be civil war. Those who desired power would use the situation as an excuse to unseat the queen, thinking it easier to undermine, influence or dethrone an inexperienced new king. "Do you think you can get your hands on another one of those scrolls?"

"I can try, but Lynnalin lives at the mage academy." The academy was near Kern's apartment, just outside the walls of the palace grounds. Going there would not be easy.

"I think it is worth the risk. We need a backup plan in case Kern's contact isn't able to get us across the border. Bradley, I know this is asking a lot, but can Frex stay here while we go get the scroll?"

"He may. The guards have already checked us, so it is unlikely they will come back again right away. He should be safe here for the time being."

Borrowing a shawl from Veronica to cover her ears and partially hide her face, Marcy and Thomas left.

Svanteese knocked on the chamber door. He heard a moan and knocked again. "Your Majesty?" When he didn't hear an answer, he pushed open the door. She may kill him for the intrusion, but the queen had missed all her morning meetings and no one knew where she was. The last anyone saw she was at the temple. Even more troubling, there was now a fourth name on the scroll of Venerith.

There was no one in the main chamber. He heard a groan in the bed chamber and hesitated. "Your Majesty?"

"Help me."

Svanteese tore open the bedroom door. Maerishka lay curled in a ball on the floor. "I'll get help."

"No," she reached up, but the movement was weak and her hand quickly fell heavily to the floor.

Svanteese thought of what to do. She obviously didn't want anyone to know she was hurt, but he needed help if he was to care for her and whatever ailment plagued her. Rushing from the room, he found her handmaiden. Azalaie was the only other person the queen trusted. She was, after all, the person who warned her of the former king and queen's plot on her life.

"She is burning up," Azalaie pulled back her hand. Unable to touch Maerishka without burning themselves, they grabbed blankets and used those to move her to the bed. Pulling out a beaded necklace Azalaie ran her hands over the beads and sang. Healing magic poured forth and surrounded the queen. When the song was done she tried again to touch her, but the result was the same. "This is not a natural illness."

"I fear she may have entered into a pact with Venerith."

Her eyes widened. "Then there is little we can do for her." Silently they set about the impossible task to make her as comfortable as possible.

Walking through the city was nerve wracking. They opted to walk in the open. No one was looking for a single elven woman traveling with a human, so they were unlikely to attract much attention. Hiding in shadows and alleys would only look suspicious, should they be seen. The festival week was about halfway over. Mindful of travel delays, visitors often arrived weeks in advance, not wanting to miss the first two days of non-stop events and activities. Normally by this time, the tourists would begin to clear out to start their long journeys home, thinning the crowds. This was not a normal year. Thousands of people of every age and race were arriving every day for the Tournament of Fire. The opening ceremonies were only one day away.

"You need to relax." Thomas took her hand as they rushed in front of a parade float to cross the street. "It's a festival. If anyone sees you looking worried or nervous, they may start to ask questions." He smiled warmly, waving to people as they passed.

"Easy for you to say," she replied through a fake smile and clenched teeth. "You aren't the one they are looking for."

"Not yet, but that could quickly change, especially if you don't loosen up." Grinning mischievously, he spun her around to the music playing from a nearby shop. "Relax," he whispered into her ear. Her worries temporarily forgotten, she stared up into his eyes. "Wait here." Ducking into the shop, Thomas came out with cake and drinks. He looked completely at ease, and she could almost pretend they were just two regular people enjoying the festival together. They ate and drank as they walked, taking in the sights and stopping to look at some of the performers. He was right, she felt much less nervous now that she was behaving normally. By the time they made it to the mage academy, she felt more like her old self.

The academy consisted of a large tree with several buildings perched on the massive limbs. The inner trunk was hollow, leaving open a chamber only accessible from the homes. The magi there were big about privacy. Lynnalin answered the door on the first knock. She wore black leather pants, a black halter top corset with bright blue flames licking up the sides and front, and fake Venerith horns strapped to her head. "Marcy, I've been looking for you. I have a birthday present."

"You didn't have to," but it was already too late. Lynnalin ran inside excitedly.

"It's your birthday?" Thomas asked.

Marcy shrugged. "I don't really celebrate it."

"You have to," Lynnalin said, returning with a small box. "It's the big two-oh-oh."

"Wait, so your birthday is at Solstice, and you're two hundred? That would make you the same age as the city," Thomas commented.

"Are you calling me old?" Marcy saw the look on his face and grinned to let him know she was teasing.

"No, I just didn't think there were any children here when the city was founded. I mean, wasn't it pretty dangerous with all the recently released criminals from Aleria?

"Marcy's parents were dangerous criminals," Lynnalin commented, her hands on Marcy's arms. Her chin rested on Marcy's shoulder.

"Lynnalin," Marcy warned, shrugging her off.

"Really?" Thomas asked, intrigued. He spoke to Lynnalin but kept his eyes on Marcy.

"Yes, they were both murderers," She leaned in and whispered conspiratorially.

"Lynn!"

"What? It's true. By the way, I'm Lynnalin." She held out her hand for Thomas to kiss. He took it but only inclined his head slightly. Marcy hid a grin at Lynnalin's slightly disappointed expression. The grin died when she saw the way Thomas glanced back at her from the corner of his eye. She knew he wanted to ask her about her parents, but he was too polite to do so in front of someone else.

"Anyway, here is your present."

Out of politeness she took the gift and opened it. Inside the box was a broach shaped like a butterfly. "It has some spells on it, but you will have to wear it to find out what they are," she winked.

"This is too much," Marcy argued. The wings gleamed of blue stones. The setting was black onyx. Even without the added magical effects, it was a generous gift.

"It's from when I needed to practice putting spells on inanimate objects. This was my test object."

"You don't know what all spells are on here, do you?" Marcy teased.

"Well, I know which ones I tried to do, but I'm not all sure what took. So enjoy, and hopefully it won't blow you up." Lynnalin followed up her comment with a big grin.

"Tell me again why I'm friends with a mage," she lamented.

"Because we're fun. Well I wish I could stick around, but I have to get going," Lynnalin announced, picking up her bag. "There is this party in the center ring of the tree for all the mages. We are going to use our spells to put on a light show." Her eyes twinkled with excitement.

"Before you go, you wouldn't happen to have any more change appearance spells I could use?" She hated to ask for something after she had just been given a gift, but that scroll was the best shot they had to get out of the city if things went wrong.

Lynnalin did not look the least disturbed by her request. "I think so," she dug into her bag. After pulling out a handful of scrolls, she found the one she needed and handed it to Marcy. "Last one. I can make some more, but it will take time."

"One is good. I really appreciate it." She hugged Lynnalin and accepted the scroll gratefully.

She felt a little strange leaving. Lynn was a good friend, and they may never see each other again. Only, she couldn't tell her that. She waved goodbye and ran down the stairs, probably thinking they would run into each other again in a day or two.

Marcy looked down at her gift and felt guilty. She replayed the entire conversation through her head. Every word had more importance and meaning when looked at through the lens of a final conversation, the last words you would ever speak to each other. Then something else about their conversation stuck out in her head. "I just realized you never told her your name, and she didn't even notice. Neither did I, for that matter."

"Sometimes anonymity has its perks."

"I can understand why you did not want to volunteer your name, but how did you do that without us noticing?" she pressed.

"It's not that difficult. People rarely pay much attention to what someone else says when they meet for the first time. Most of your focus is going to be on yourself and what you are saying. People are inherently a little self-centered. Some are more so than others, but we all have that tendency that is easy to exploit if you know how to do it."

They came to a crossroads. The path north led back to Bradley and Veronica's home. The path west led to her home and her brother's tavern. She almost took the westward path out of habit. How many times had she walked that way, she wondered. Three hundred steps down the tree lined road would take her to a curve. Another few hundred feet and she would be able to hear the excitement from the racetrack. She could see every tree, every road, every home and business. At the end of her walk would be her brother. Before she could imagine what she would say, Thomas took her hand and started down the westward path. "What are you doing?"

"You have someone you need to say 'goodbye' to." It wasn't a question.

"My brother," she answered. He began walking again. "Wait, we can't. There's no time, and besides, they will be looking for me there."

Thomas turned to face her, smiling warmly. He still held her hand. "We can't do anything until morning, so time is not an issue, and let me worry about the guards. Neither of us knows what awaits us tomorrow. You should see your brother." Without waiting for her response, he led her home.

"I told you this was a bad idea." Marcy and Thomas hid just inside the tree line across the street from her brother's tavern. Royal Guards kept coming and going. It wasn't completely uncommon for guards to eat at the tavern, but these guards were much too alert to be simply enjoying an evening meal or drink. Every time the door opened, she could see her brother talking to one. He did not seem pleased. No doubt by now he was cursing her for whatever trouble she was in that could bring down the attention of the crown on his tavern. With all the business they were doing for the holiday, he would be angry with the distraction.

"We'll think of something," Thomas assured her. "Maybe I can go in and talk to him, get him to come out."

Marcy looked at him doubtfully. The guards would probably still be hovering around the bar. They needed a way to communicate to Bryce without arousing suspicion. "I have an idea." She pulled out a sheet of parchment and began folding it. Within seconds, she held a white flower in her hands. Thomas whistled in appreciation. "Get Bryce's attention and put the flower on the counter. Once you know he has seen it, tell him you want to order your usual and ask if he can deliver it. Then meet me at the big tree by the park."

Thomas took the flower and disappeared inside the tavern. Not waiting for him to come out, Marcy made her way to the rendezvous point.

"It didn't work. He didn't get the message." Marcy paced around in front of the tree.

"It's only been a half hour. Why don't you come and sit down?" Thomas patted the ground next to him and waited for her to comply.

"Are you sure he saw the flower?"

"Yes, he did a double take and looked at me very intently before one of the guards looked over, and he had to hide his reaction." Marcy sighed and sat back, resting her head on his shoulder. "What's the story behind the flower, anyway?"

Marcy was quiet for so long he thought she would not answer. Finally, she spoke, her voice tinged with reflection and a hint of resigned sadness. "Bryce and I did not always get along. We have the same father but different mothers. He never approved of my mother and was angry with our father for remarrying. At first he tried to separate them, but after I was born, he knew that would be impossible. He told me once that the day I was born was the second worst day of his life."

"Which is why you don't celebrate your birthday," he surmised.

Marcy nodded. "When I was a child I would pick white roses that grew near our house and bring them to him as a kind of peace offering. It started out slowly at first, a rose here or there when he was particularly angry. Then I decided to bring him a flower every day until he accepted me. It went on for a month before he told me I could stop. We've been fairly close ever since."

"What happened to his mother?" Thomas knew it was nosey, but he couldn't help asking. Elves tended to mate for life, so half siblings and step parents were not as common as with other races. It was little wonder he would have difficulty dealing with his father remarrying.

"She was murdered." Thomas sat up a little straighter, his arm tightening reflexively. "It wasn't my father, if that is what you're wondering." Thomas didn't answer, but his guilty eyes gave him away. "It was a robbery gone wrong."

"But he did kill someone?" he couldn't help asking.

"You say that as though it were a bad thing. How many people have you killed?"

Thomas understood her confusion. The Flame Guard had a reputation for certain unsavory activities. Many were little more than hired thugs, ready to do anything and everything for the right amount of gold. "We can refuse any job, even one issued by the crown. I avoid those jobs that would require me to kill."

"You killed those guards at Kern's place."

"I didn't say I couldn't kill or that I hadn't killed before, just that I avoid it when possible. Who did your father kill?"

"Well, as I said before, my father's first wife was killed in a robbery. It was back in Aleria during the Time of Black Law. They found the person responsible, but he had connections and a deep coin purse. He was released without punishment. My father tracked him down and killed him. Of course they arrested my father, and he spent over ten years in prison before the purge. While in prison, he met someone, a woman convicted of killing her would be rapist. It just so happened he was also a prominent judge. No one believed her story and she was thrown in jail on a life sentence. After the purge, they married and I was conceived. They chose to move to Suriax, saying they didn't trust the law to punish those who needed it. They wanted to live somewhere they could defend themselves and their family." Marcy's chin tilted up defiantly, daring him to find something wrong with her story or the choices her family made. The flicker of doubt in her eyes belied her challenging gaze. She was conflicted, though she would likely never admit it. The daughter of two killers, how else could she view this story but to believe them completely justified? Yet her eyes told a different story. She may love her parents and even understand why they did what they did, but something inside her doubted her conviction and beliefs. Thomas didn't know what to say.

Would he make a different choice in their circumstances? Luckily he didn't have to answer that unasked question. Bryce chose that moment to appear at the edge of the clearing. Marcy rose and went to him, wrapping her brother in a warm hug. He hugged her back and immediately started grilling her for answers to what was going on. Thomas listened from the tree, not wanting to intrude on their conversation.

"What have you gotten yourself into? I've had guards squatting at the tavern since last night. If not for all the idiot tourists, I'd have no business at all. The locals are steering clear."

"I know I'm sorry about that. I can't go into the details, but it is serious. They are looking for Kern. I was watching his uncle, so now they are looking for me, hoping I can lead them to Kern."

"Can you?" Marcy looked away, biting her lip. "You have to tell them. Maybe then they will leave us alone."

"Bryce," she chided.

"I'm serious. I like him as much as you, but you do not want to mess with these people. If Kern is in trouble, he can get out of it, or not, himself. It is better to keep to yourself and not get their attention. Trust me. You do not want powerful people coming after you."

"I can't. This is too important. Bryce, I am leaving the city, and I don't know if I'm coming back."

"What? You are acting crazy. Are you that much in love with the man that you would throw your life away for him?"

"I'm not in love with Kern," she said, shocked he would suggest such a thing.

"Why else would you do all this?"

"Because it's the right thing to do!"

They both took a breath, allowing their tempers to subside before either spoke again. "Where are you going?" Bryce asked at last.

"Aleria."

"Yeah, well, don't get yourself killed. Here," he handed her a 'to go' box from the tavern. "Some food for the road."

Marcy took the box, letting her hand linger on his. Bryce shot Thomas a pointed look but didn't ask who he was. Marcy didn't volunteer anything either. The less he knew, the better for everyone. She held the box and watched Bryce leave.

CHAPTER FIVE

KERN STRUGGLED AGAINST THE GUARDS' HOLD, TRYING TO EXPLAIN himself. Sneaking into the palace had seemed like a good idea at the time. Okay, so it never seemed like a good idea, but what choice did he have? Getting an audience with the Kings or Queen was not that easy, especially when the guards learned he was from Suriax. He was lucky he hadn't been deported on the spot. He couldn't really blame them. It did look suspicious. Why would anyone from Suriax need to speak to the royal family? They had to protect their monarchs. There were other ways to get messages through, and given enough time he could possibly even get them to arrange a meeting, but he didn't have that kind of time, and it would require telling too many people who he was. So, he broke in. Everything would have gone fine, but they had anti-magic wards around the queen's chambers that picked up on his magical items and alerted the guards the moment he passed the threshold.

"What is going on here?" A woman dressed in a robe and nightgown entered from one of the other rooms in the suite.

"Your Majesty, I apologize for the disturbance. We were just removing this law breaker. He broke into the palace and your room, Milady."

Kern looked at the woman before him and recognized her instantly from her picture. Many years passed since the portrait was painted, but there was no mistaking her identity. This was his sister. "Queen Mirerien, I need to talk to you. My name is Kern Tygi …"

"You are aware that breaking into the palace is a crime?" she asked, cutting him off.

"Yes, but …"

"Take him away." With a dismissive wave, she turned to go.

"I'm your brother!"

Mirerien stopped short and turned back to face him, studying him intently. The guards waited dutifully for her response. "Even if that were somehow true, it would be no reason for breaking the law. There are proper channels and procedures to go through."

"Wow, you are just as he described."

"Who?"

"Uncle Frex."

Her previously controlled, emotionless demeanor melted away. "Frex? I thought he died."

"Not yet, but he isn't much longer for this world. That's actually what brought me here. To keep me safe, he's been living in a self-imposed exile all these years. I wanted to bring him home before it's too late."

Mirerien looked off, lost in thought. Sensing her change, the guards relaxed their hold on Kern, looking at each other uncertainly. "Your Majesty?"

The guards questioning tone snapped her back to the present. "Release him. You may go," she dismissed them. Waiting for the guards to leave, Mirerien poured a couple of drinks, offering one to Kern. He accepted, eyeing the ruby liquid somewhat dubiously. He didn't recognize the name on the bottle, but even he could tell it was expensive, likely worth as much as he made in a year. Taking a slow drink he could appreciate its quality, but he knew he wouldn't get used to it any time soon. He was more of a one copper piece ale drinker. It was a little unsettling to realize how his entire personality, who he was, what he thought, how he looked at the world could have been so very different if he had been raised here in the palace of Aleria instead of a small rundown apartment in Suriax. He could have been a completely different person. Maybe his mother knew what she was doing after all.

"Where is Frex, now?" she asked at last.

"Suriax. That's where we've been living."

Her face screwed up in disdain at the mention of Suriax. He felt the absurd urge to defend his home, but this wasn't the time. He had other things to attend to first. "I'm loath to move him. Suriax has been his home for over two centuries, but someone found out about me, and I'm worried it may not be safe there any longer. I came here to see if he would be welcome were he to come here."

"Of course he would. He is family."

"I don't mean to insult you," he added quickly in response to her tone. "To be fair, I don't know any of you. I didn't even know we were related until a couple of days ago. Frex never told me any of this. As far as I'm concerned, he is my only family, and I won't do anything to hurt him or bring him any pain. If I'm about to ask him to leave his home, I'm going to make damn sure he's going to an even better one, with people who will care for him and treat him right. If you can promise me that place is here, I will take you at your word. If not, let me know now, and I will make my plans to keep him safe there."

Her face softened, whatever doubts she still had of his identity laid to rest by his heartfelt defense of Frex. "I fear I never cared for him as deeply as you apparently do. I could claim youthful ignorance, but that would only be an excuse. I have dedicated my entire life to the law, and I do not regret that, but I fear it has left me rather cold to others."

"Sister, are you alright?" The door opened, two men in their night tunics rushing in. They stopped short at seeing Kern. "So this is your visitor?" one of them said. They eyed Kern suspiciously. Their hands held sheathed swords, the securing leather straps hanging loose, evidence of the speed with which they made their way to her chamber.

"You can put those away," Mirerien said, indicating the swords. "As you can see, I'm in no danger. Now, say 'hello' to Kern, our brother."

"So what are we going to do about our dear brother?" Eirae leaned against the door-jam with his arms crossed in front of him.

"What do you mean?" Mirerien poured three glasses of tea and handed them out.

"You had to have noticed his jacket."

"Mirerien never pays attention to the goings on in Suriax," Pielere replied. "It was the jacket of the Flame Guard," he informed her.

"The Flame Guard?" her eyes widened in distress.

"Hence the need to figure out what we are going to do about him." Eirae stepped away from the door. "Can we trust him?"

"He is our brother," Pielere set his glass down.

"And Veritan was our father. Maerishka is our half-sister," he rebutted. "Before we go trusting him, we need to know he hasn't been corrupted beyond redemption, as they were."

"How do you propose we do that? I can only say if he tells the truth. I can't predict the future." She gathered the glasses and returned them to their tray.

Eirae's eyes narrowed in thought. "I need to question him," he answered. The other two shared a look. He wasn't known for his kindness in gathering information, but he was good at drawing out the darkness in a man's heart. If someone was guilty of a crime, a few minutes alone with Eirae were usually enough to bring out a confession. He knew how to get the job done. "If he's with the guard, he will have killed. We need to ascertain his feelings about that. If he is corrupted on that issue, all others are moot."

"He did come all this way for our uncle. That is not something our father would have done." Pielere gave a hopeful look.

"And what of Uncle Frex?" asked Mirerien. "He has lived in Suriax with Kern all this time."

"I don't think we need to worry about Frex." Eirae patted his sister on the shoulder. "He had no love for our father or Venerith. He was a close friend of grandfather's after all."

"Father, Father!" Two small boys ran in, jumping on Pielere's lap.

"Hey, what are you two doing up?" He tousled their hair.

"We heard there is a new guest in the palace," the older boy answered. "Is it true?"

The three Alerian lords looked at each other. Eirae shrugged. "There's no keeping secrets in a palace." Squatting down in front of the children, he looked at them warmly. "We do have a guest."

"Can we meet him?" the younger boy asked.

"Probably, but not tonight."

"Awww," they complained.

"You heard your uncle." Pielere slid them to their feet and stood. "It's time to go back to sleep. Come on, I'll go with you."

"I think we could all use some sleep," Mirerien agreed. They had many things to discuss, but for once, they could wait until the morning.

Thomas could not wait for morning. After hours of avoiding guards, he was exhausted. They made it back to the house, but now he could not sleep. He still needed to talk to Kern, finalize plans for tomorrow and keep watch in case the guards came back. He twisted the ring around his finger and waited for Kern to reply. A few minutes later, he heard Kern's voice whisper softly in his head. "What is the plan?" he asked back.

"I made contact," Kern answered. "There will be someone waiting for you once you cross the gate, but they can't send him over into Suriax without alerting the queen to your presence and causing some potential political complications. Of course, if things change and you are in eminent danger, let me know and they will send their man across the border."

"Understood."

"I should probably explain what is going on."

"No need. You uncle already filled us in."

There was an audible sigh on Kern's end. "I never meant for either of you to get caught up in all this."

"It's alright. I didn't really want to stay in Suriax forever, anyway."

"I'm so sorry. I never thought you both would have to leave Suriax, too. I just wanted to get my uncle to safety.

"Things happen for a reason." Thomas heard a board creak by the kitchen. "Got to go." He twisted the ring to end the conversation and went to check out the sound. He found Marcy standing on the back porch, staring at the night sky. She wore a long cotton gown. Her hair was down for the first time since they met. Long golden locks fell down her back, well past her waist. As he watched, she pulled a brush through her hair. He turned to leave.

"I missed the sunset," she said without turning. "I thought I'd make it out here in time to see the sun set over Suriax one last time, but I failed to compensate for the trees around here. My apartment and the tavern have a more open view of the skyline."

"I'm sorry."

"It's alright." She turned to face him, her hair falling gracefully around her. "I don't feel the same fondness for Suriax that you showed when you described your home. What I feel is more akin to nostalgia. Truthfully, I don't think I'll miss it all that much. I just wonder how well I would actually fit in anywhere else. I may not care all that much for Suriax, but it is a large part of who I am. Living here has shaped my opinions and personality. I've tried to put myself in your position, to see killing as you do, but I'm a recorder. For over a hundred years, death has been little more to me than a few facts on a scroll; name, age and why did you kill him? I had forgotten that isn't how it is viewed everywhere else. How am I supposed to be a part of that outside world that would shun and mistrust me should they learn of my origins?" She turned around, her hair whipping around in her haste. "I'm sorry. I know you don't have the answer to my questions. I'll be inside in a bit. I'd like to have some time alone to think first. Goodnight."

Feeling a bit helpless, Thomas mumbled a "Goodnight," and went inside.

The streets were overflowing with people, performers and vendors. Confetti filled the air. Acrobats jumped and swung from trees. There were fire eaters, very popular in Suriax, given that Venerith was a god of law and fire. It was said his fire burned through the sentimentality of laws that became distracted with notions of right and wrong. His laws were pure, true laws. Those who did not follow his teachings called this school of thought perverse, but it was the basis for all Suriaxian society, and they believed in him completely.

The crowds were particularly thick near the stadium. Everyone was excited about the opening of the Tournament of Fire. Younger, rookie competitors bragged about previous victories. Veteran contestants, especially previous finalists, were surrounded by fans. People screamed just to be heard. In the distance a band played, adding to the cacophony of sounds. You couldn't actually make out what they were playing until they played a trio of notes everyone from Suriax recognized. As one the crowd began singing the Suriaxian anthem, "The Blue Flame of Purity." Blue fire was nearly the hottest fire there was. It was also the color of Venerith's flame, for only the hottest fire could burn to the truth. They sang of being reborn in the blue flame, set free from the morality of others' laws. They thanked Venerith for their blessings and prayed for Suriax to remain strong and true. When the song ended there was a reverent moment of silence, deafening after the loudness that had preceded it. Someone cheered and the crowd followed.

Horns blared from the top of the stadium tree, announcing the start of the tournament. Contestants buzzed with excitement, leading their respective entourages inside. Banners flew through the air. The inside of the stadium tree was even more heavily decorated than the rest of the festival. Performers danced and did acrobatic flips along rafter-like tree branches running through the main stadium room. The walls swirled around in an impossible design, curving to allow seating, both common and special reserved balconies. The sky was visible through a canopy of limbs and leaves, moonlight casting a magical glow on the room and everyone in it. The competitors took to the floor, beginning their warm ups and demonstrations of their skill, while the audience filed in and took their seats. Roaming food vendors sold Vaxtamil ale and various snacks. The horns blared again, signaling the start of the exhibition fights. The previous tournament's winner and runner up took to the stage. The audience cheered. Ten years earlier, Zanden, a rookie contestant in his first tournament, blew everyone away by making it to the final round. In the end, he was defeated by the previous champion, Sardon Barief. Their match went on for three days with only brief breaks for food to carry them through. Their rematch was one of the most highly anticipated of the tournament. Even though this was technically just an exhibition fight, everyone knew it was so much more than that. As a three time champion, Sardon could not participate in the full tournament this year. After three wins, contestants were forced to retire from competing to allow other competitors to rise to the top. In rare cases a former retired champ was asked to return for a special match up, but that was only ever against another three time champion. This was Zanden's last shot for the foreseeable future to fight Sardon and prove who was superior. Both men had much to lose and gain through victory.

Without preamble, they began to fight. For several long minutes the only sounds to be heard in the stadium were grunts at well placed punches, feet slapping against the ground, fists hitting flesh and the even sounds of their breathing. Even the vendors fell silent. Everyone sat in anticipation of who would draw first blood.

Maerishka heard a knock at the door of her balcony and motioned for her attendants to answer it. They looked at each other uncertainly, neither wanting to miss a moment of this fight. At the second knock, a young female attendant lost the battle of wills and begrudgingly answered the door, admitting King Alvexton. Maerishka bowed slightly and gestured for him to join her.

"Your Highness, you look lov …. ly." Alvexton's eyes widened as he caught sight of the flame markings going up the right of Maerishka's neck and face. Purposefully, she handed him her marked hand. To his credit, he took it, placing a kiss directly on one of the flame marks.

"Your Highness," she returned in kind, speaking softly to avoid distracting people from the fight. "I'm pleased you could make it tonight."

"I missed you at the celebrations the past two days."

Maerishka smiled apologetically. The first day after her pact was made, she could barely move from the pain. Once that subsided, she felt stronger, more energetic, but she still did not know what to do about her markings. What, if anything, should she reveal to her subjects? Should she hide them from her visitors? Royals and lords were notoriously easy to spook when other leaders gained a substantial amount of power. Blessing from a god would definitely fall into that category. She did not want to scare any of her trade partners away or provoke a fearful attack. And if anyone found out why she made her bargain, it could mean the end of her reign. She needed to handle this situation carefully to avoid unwanted consequences. Finally, she opted to wear them proudly. Should anyone have the guts to question her about them, she would say they were a blessing from Venerith. That was all anyone needed to know. If she was too afraid to show the markings she did not deserve to have them. "Are you familiar at all with the Tournament of Fire?" she asked.

"I've heard of it of course, but I've never had the pleasure to witness it. Is it true it only comes around once a decade?"

"That is correct, however, we do hold many other competitions and smaller tournaments regularly. They are usually only for locals. The Tournament of Fire invites people from all over the continent to participate. Winning is a very high honor."

The crowd cheered and Maerishka turned her attention back to the match. Zanden was performing very well. She would need to keep her eye on him.

"Just sit tight. We will be on the way soon." The merchant dropped the blanket covering the produce on his wagon, leaving Thomas, Marcy and Frex in darkness. The wagon was specially designed for transporting restricted items. It had a false bottom with a hidden compartment roughly six feet long by five feet wide. It was only deep enough to allow a person to lie flat, and to fit all three of them, Marcy had to lie halfway on top of Thomas, not that either of them really minded. There were narrow slits cut for air holes spread throughout, though most were covered by the produce and blanket. A couple along the sides allowed them sporadic views of people walking by.

They waited in silence for what felt like hours. Just when Marcy was about to fall asleep from boredom, the wagon would jar them by roughly rolling over the uneven, graveled road. Hinges and tools clanged loudly in their ears. Whenever that happened, Thomas would tighten his arms around her, bracing them both against the movement. Instinctively, she would reach an arm out to do the same for Frex. For his age, he handled the rough journey well, without complaint. After a few stops and starts, the wagon settled into an even pace. She was about to fall back to sleep when she felt a tap on her shoulder. Thomas motioned silently to the air slot by his head and grinned. Scooting up a few inches, Marcy squinted to look through the narrow opening. Purple and pink covered the sky. It was sunset. Looking back at Thomas, their faces barely an inch apart, she felt a tear roll down her cheek. She looked back out at the sunset until all the colors faded into darkness. Then she sighed and laid her head on Thomas' chest, letting herself sleep at last.

Maerishka wiped the sweat from her brow, grabbing a fan to cool off. The stadium wasn't usually so warm, especially not at night. The roof was open to the sky, allowing in a breeze. She saw the flags wave, but the wind did not have any effect on her. Looking around, she noticed no one else seemed bothered by the temperature. They were all focused on the exhibition match still raging between Zanden and Sardon. It was then she realized it was not coming from outside. The heat was coming from inside her. Struggling to retain her composure she moved to stand, knocking over a glass of water in the process. Alvexton and the guards looked at her questionably. "I'm afraid I've had a bit too much excitement for the night. There is still so much to do tomorrow to prepare for the final royal gala. But I've had a lovely time with you, tonight."

"Of course, I understand completely" Alvexton replied. "I as well have enjoyed your company. I look forward to seeing you tomorrow." Bowing, he took his leave.

Maerishka dismissed her guards and retreated to her private chamber adjoining the balcony. Opulent, even by royal standards, it held many marvels. The stadium was built with strong magic out of three hundred foot wide tree. The walls and doors were all part of the tree that were manipulated to curve around and grow in such a way to create hollow spaces for rooms. Most were simple, yet still awe inspiring. Her room was a step above all that. The wood of the tree curved to create her furniture. The tables, chairs and bed were all part of the tree. Moss and leaves formed cushions and the mattress. A moss carpet covered the floor, and leaves fanned out around a small sky light. Flowers decorated the room, adding their fragrance and beauty to complete the scene.

But she didn't notice any of that now. The burning was a raging inferno, worse than anything she imagined, even after her encounter with the statue. Through her pain, she sensed a presence behind her. A man, no not a man, but Venerith himself stepped out of the shadows. Staggering in height, his horns brushed against the fifteen foot ceiling. Seeing his statue did nothing to prepare her for seeing him in person. Thick horns curled from behind his head around above his eyes. Two long horns protruded from his chin, surrounded by three shorter ones on either side. Together, they formed a sharp bone beard. In fact, all the hair on his face was formed from bone. His eyebrows were a series of small spikes and a row of short horns ran along the center of his head. Venerith's skin was a glossy black. It was so black, if one looked at it too long, you could imagine other colors lost within the darkness. He wore a blue leather tunic with white accents forming flames across the surface. A strap holding scrolls as one may carry knives crossed over his chest and around his back. Large clawed hands carried a larger scroll and a weapon that resembled a scepter. It was actually a large mace with a shaft the length of a staff. The top held an ornate globe of swirling colors lost in a black field of darkness. The setting for the globe was three curved blades. Blue flames ran up the length of the otherwise black shaft. It was as beautiful as it was dangerous. Where he walked, smoke appeared, leaving scorch marks on the floor. A faint aura of fire surrounded him without obscuring his appearance or burning the scrolls. His eyes were bright blue glowing orbs of light. It was impossible to tell where he looked, though she could feel the focus of his attention completely on her. He was beautiful and terrifying in his intensity.

She wondered, as she writhed in agony, what she did to displease him. Why was he punishing her like this? Maybe he had changed his mind and was canceling their agreement. Maybe he did not think her worthy of his blessings. Finally, unable and afraid to vocalize all her questions and fears, she spoke the only word she could think to speak. "Why?"

He grinned and squatted down beside her. "Power doesn't come without a price." He touched her chin and she went blind from the pain. When her vision returned, she almost wished it hadn't. Flames surrounded her entire body. Heat infused her eyeballs, the hairs on her head, even her toenails burned. It was as if her body was made of fire and not skin and blood and muscle. The fire was her strength. Her blood was molten heat. Her skin was just the visible edge of the flame. The flames ebbed and flowed with her breaths. She was fire. Slowly, the flames pulled back into her skin, the heat simmering beneath the surface. Whether the heat subsided or her tolerance of it was increased, she did not know, but the pain lessened as well. Finally, she felt the pain ease away entirely. Feeling stronger than ever before, she held out her hands and called the flames to her. They came at once. This time, she did not burn. They grew and dissipated at her command. Excitement filled her.

This was power unlike any she dared hope for. Surely no one could ever challenge her, now. She was invincible.

A scream sounded outside. She ignored it, but it was followed by others. Standing, she went to the balcony. In the stands and the floor of the stadium, people doubled over in pain. One by one, they were surrounded by flames. Her eyes teared, her body shook in fury. This wasn't fair. She was the one who made the bargain. She and she alone was the one who should have received Venerith's blessing.

Venerith walked up behind her and put a clawed hand casually on her shoulder. "Now, now, you didn't think you were special, did you?" He chuckled and faded back into the shadows.

CHAPTER SIX

THE GRASS WAS COOL ON HER BARE FEET. MIRERIEN PULLED BACK on her bow and let the arrow fly. The arrow wobbled from the force with which it hit the target. She closed her eyes and felt the cool night air blow across her cheek.

"You don't usually train so late." Collin stepped out from behind the weapon's shed and sat on a raised tree root. Casually, he began to sharpen his blade.

"This has been an unusual day."

"So I've heard."

"What have you heard?" Mirerien put her bow down sat beside him on the root.

"That a Flame Guardsman broke into your room and claimed to be your long lost brother."

"I see the gossips are working overtime."

"So it isn't true?"

"No, your source is correct. He has been living in Suriax with an uncle we thought dead."

"So you got a brother and an uncle all in one day. That is incredible."

The sounds of night insects filled the quiet training yard. Mirerien dangled a foot down to rub against the grass.

Moonlight beamed down and cast a subtle blue hue on everything. Without thinking she asked the question paramount on her mind. "Do you think I am cold?" The moment the words left her mouth, she regretted them. Collin looked taken aback by the question. "Never mind." Standing, she grabbed her bow and took her stance.

"Your shoulders are too high. You need to relax them." Collin put his hands around her shoulders and rubbed them until they loosened up. "Why do you think you are cold?"

"I don't know how I should feel."

"You should feel how you feel."

Mirerien turned to face him, not as uncomfortable by the intimacy of their proximity as she thought she would be. "I want to smile."

Collin laughed. "Then smile. It's not that hard."

"Pielere says I smile more when I am with you." Collin's face grew serious, his stare intense. She thought they might kiss, but movement caught her eye and ended the moment. Bright blue streaks of light shot through the sky. Most disappeared far off into the distance, but a few did not. Several hit the palace. Then she heard the screams.

The sound of yelling, both excited and fearful, awoke Kern from his dreamless sleep. Stumbling to the hall, he had to jump back into his room to avoid being hit by people running past his door. There was a dim, blue glow on everything, blue light shining in through the windows, each one surrounded by frantic people trying to get a look. Kern didn't bother stopping, instead he headed for the courtyard on the second floor balcony of the palace. Absentmindedly he noticed the other people already out there, but he couldn't have said who they were. His attention was focused on the sky. Large balls of blue, white and black fire burned through the air, landing squarely on the shores of Suriax. From his vantage point, he couldn't see much, but it looked as though the entire city was on fire. Smaller fires dotted Aleria, most confined to the Market Square shared with Suriax. He worried for his uncle. Thomas and Marcy were to travel across the border around nightfall. Assuming everything went as planned they should be safe in Aleria by now. As soon as he returned to his room, he would get the ring and contact them again to be sure.

As he watched, a burning sensation began in his belly, building, spreading throughout his body until he felt sure he was on fire. He was vaguely aware of crying out. His vision turned to white, blinded by an impossibly bright light. The burning increased to levels he hadn't believed possible. A small spot in his vision cleared. Looking down at his hands, he found them covered in blue flames.

Kern heard singing and smiled. He often dreamed of waking up to the beautiful sound of a woman, his woman, singing. Children would be laughing in some other room of the house. The smell of freshly cooked meat and bread would fill the air. But it was only a dream. That was not the life he had. There was no wife and certainly no children. So who could be singing now? The last thing he remembered … panic flooded through him as he remembered the blue flames engulfing his hands. Sitting up, he inspected them closely, expecting burns. There were none. His hands looked the same as always. How could that be? He saw them burning. He felt the heat.

"It's alright." Marcy put her hands over his.

"What happened, and why do I feel I was beat upside the head with a brick?"

She crinkled her nose. "That's not too far from the truth. During all the excitement last night, you fell and hit your head on the bricks lining the garden outside. You managed to knock a corner off one of them," she grinned. "I always knew you had a hard head. Now I have proof."

Kern rubbed his head, feeling the knot there. "Very funny. So, what was all that?"

"As far as any of us can figure, it had to do with the Solstice celebrations. Only Suriaxians were affected."

"Uncle?"

"Is fine. He wasn't born in Suriax, and he never changed his citizenship from Aleria. That seems to be the determining factor. Thomas wasn't affected either."

"Then you …"

Marcy pulled back her hair to reveal a dark marking in the shape of a flame at the back of her neck. "We all have one." His hand went instinctively to his neck. "And we can all do this." She held out a hand and blue flames immediately covered it. Kern jumped, but she was unconcerned, not a flinch. Waiting a few moments, she closed her hand. The flames went out instantly. "I was hit just after we crossed the border. The merchant barely got the cover off the wagon and pulled Frex out before I set the thing on fire. Thomas got a few burns trying to put me out. Then we heard the other screams and saw the fires in Suriax and figured out what was happening. The merchant ran off as soon as we were all out of the wagon. It was a good thing the palace sent someone to meet us, or we would have had to walk the entire way here." She gave a weak grin and laugh. The skin around her eyes was creased with lack of sleep and worry. Kern put a hand on her arm and she instantly stiffened, pulling back. "Now that you're up, I should go check on how Thomas is doing with his burns. Frex is down at the end of the hall." Standing abruptly, she left.

"Now you hide."

He could hear children laugh excitedly, followed by a deep

chuckle. "I may be a little big for most of the hiding places in here," Frex said. "How about you hide again for me, and I'll find you?"

The children agreed, and Frex began counting. After he finished, the giggling continued. Kern looked in to see Frex and four small children who weren't really what you could call hidden. One was under a table, one hid squatting in a corner with his hands covering his face and one was in the middle of the floor with a blanket half covering her body. Her feet were still visible and kicking. The best hidden was an older boy hiding behind a planter, but even he was giggling, easily giving away his position. Frex stalked around the room, grinning from ear to ear and pretending to not know where they were.

"He looks to be having a good time. They all do in fact."

Kern jumped. Pielere stood behind him, looking in on the children. "Yes, I haven't seen Uncle this happy in years," Kern replied.

"We should leave them to it, then. Come take a walk with me." Pielere gestured down the hall. They walked to the courtyard. Kern noticed, not for the first time, the looks people shot him as he passed. They didn't trust him. They didn't like him. Some outright hated him. He noticed some of this hostility before, but it was worse now, since the night of blue fire. That is what the servants were calling it. His palms burned at the thought. He took a deep breath to calm himself before the flames could manifest themselves. It took him several hours of practicing after Marcy's visit, but he finally had some control over the flames. Unfortunately, it was not before he set fire to his jacket. He had really liked that coat, too. "How are you enjoying it here?"

"Honestly," Kern paused, not wanting to insult anyone, "I'm not sure I really belong here."

"You know you are welcome to stay as long as you like."

"I think a few of your subjects may disagree with you on that."

Pielere noticed a servant girl hurry past them, watching Kern suspiciously from the corner of her eye. He nodded. "Suriax is not very popular with most Alerians."

"But why? You guys are all about laws. So are we. We just follow different laws from you, but we still have order. I know most people don't agree with our laws allowing murder, but everything is regulated and documented, and random killings aren't that common. You aren't going to get killed just walking down the street, at least no more than anywhere else."

Pielere sighed and paused by a helephor plant at the edge of the garden. It was a large red plant, easily standing four feet tall with long, bell shaped petals. The inside of each petal was orange and yellow, and the smell it produced was strong and sweet. It was typically found along the edges of the cliffs by the sea, at the far side of the continent, and did not normally grow in this climate. This one was thriving. Behind it stood five more. It was one more example of the different world his siblings lived in. Pielere continued, oblivious to Kern's distraction. "When did you join the Flame Guard? I recognized your jacket," he explained at Kern's surprise.

Kern thought for a minute. "I was pretty young, about ninety three, I think." Had it really been that long?

"And in that time, how many people have you killed?"

"A thousand, maybe more." Pielere's eyes widened. "But it was all perfectly legal," Kern hastened to add.

"And what of the families of those you killed?"

Kern shrugged. "It was always a job or an order, so if they had a problem with it, they would most likely go after whoever ordered the kill. Or they could just kill me in response. Either way, no laws are broken and order is maintained."

"There are man's laws and god's laws. Regardless of what laws are passed and what may be legal in one land or another, there is still such a thing as right and wrong. Man's laws are supposed to exist to protect and enforce god's laws, to protect people. Otherwise they are just arbitrary means of acquiring and maintaining power."

"But our laws are a god's laws. They are from Venerith."

"There is a reason we call Venerith the Corruptor. His ways sound good. He plays to our sense of reason. But he ignores the spirit behind the law, the real reason for laws. Our father was twisted to believe laws existed for his benefit, that it was okay for him to exploit loopholes, make up excuses to fine and imprison innocent people and do all this in the name of the law. Grandfather understood his role as leader and protector of the people. He understood the responsibility of his position, the sacrifices he must make and how every one of his actions could have a real impact on the lives of those he ruled over. He took his responsibilities seriously, and so do we. We do not lead for our benefit. We lead for those who depend on us for their protection." Pielere fell silent, his head tilted to the side as though he was listening to something.

"Are you alright?" Kern asked when he didn't say anything else.

"Hmm? Oh, yes. I do apologize for that."

"What happened?"

"It's nothing. It's just that sometimes I think I hear voices." Kern raised an eyebrow. "I know. It sounds crazy."

"No, not crazy at all. And what exactly do these voices tell you to do?" He took a step back in mock fear.

Pielere laughed. "They don't tell me to do anything. They ask for help, mostly."

"Help?"

"Yes, I guess I spend too much time ruling on cases. I'm starting to hear made up ones in my head. There was one a few days ago, a woman, asking for justice for her family. She talked about a grandson forced to work for her landlord to keep their rent from being raised."

Kern felt his jaw go slack. "That is no hallucination. I met that woman on my way here. She runs a small bakery. Their old landlord died, and his son takes advantage of their lack of written contracts to force the residents into his service. If they don't, he raises the rent beyond their ability to pay."

Pielere took it all in, not looking as surprised as Kern felt. He could tell Pielere already felt the voices were real. This news just gave him the proof he needed to allow himself to believe in them. "Thank you for the information. I will see the situation is resolved right away."

"Your Majesty," a small gnome girl ran up to them. In truth she was probably at least a hundred years old, but her small size and spritely features gave the illusion of added youth. Pielere gestured for her to go on. "There are more reports of violence in the market and along the border near the bridge; twenty more robbery attempts and four more killings. Another ten people are being tended to for their injuries, mostly burns."

"Send three more squadrons out to patrol and bring in any of the perpetrators. Also see what you can do to secure more ranskie plants to treat the burns. The clerics are probably running low by now."

"Yes, Sir." She bowed and left just as quickly.

"What is going on?" Kern asked.

"I'm afraid the events of last night have left quite a mark. There have been riots breaking out everywhere. Most of Suriax is on fire or has been in the past twelve hours. We've been hit by an influx of frightened tourists and quite a few Suriaxians who believe they can now ignore our treaties and do whatever they wish. We're almost ready to close down the border. Travel between the cities is already being partially restricted. You should probably stay around the palace, at least until things calm down."

Kern caught another sideways glance from a servant and agreed Pielere was probably right, but he couldn't just sit around doing nothing. "Maybe I can help. I am a guard, after all. I could do some patrols."

Pielere looked at him uncertainly. "I don't know. You aren't an Alerian citizen. I'm not really at liberty to assign you to such a task. But," he cut Kern off when he would have argued, "you are free to come and go as you please, so what you do with that freedom is up to you. Of course, I can also point out there will be guards posted on every block near the border bridge, so if one were to see anything troubling occurring, it would be easy to report said activity." Kern grinned. "On that note, I must get back to work. Keep out of trouble," he called over his shoulder as he left.

Laureen felt her heart beating out of her chest. Kern was the rouge guardsman. He didn't seem to recognize her when she walked past him talking to King Pielere. Then again they didn't know each other all that well, and he had a lot on his mind. So did she. Unconsciously, her hand went to her neck. She could still see the looks of fear on their faces. Why did she choose to go out last night? If she had gone to bed as usual, no one would know, but they were talking about Kern and his relationship to the royal family. She wanted to learn as much as she could to report back to the queen.

"Laureen, isn't it?"

She stopped and turned to Queen Mirerien. She had anticipated this meeting all morning, though she thought an advisor or staff member would be the one to question her. "Yes, Your Majesty."

"You are Suriaxian." It wasn't a question. After last night, there was no denying it.

"Yes, Ma'am."

"Why did you not disclose this when you came to work for the palace?"

Laureen panicked. It was said no one could lie to the queen. "I was ordered not to," she lowered her eyes.

"Who gave this order?"

"I cannot say."

"I see. You know you cannot stay here any longer?" The queen did not seem angry or upset, but she was not known for her displays of emotion. It was disconcerting. Anger she could deal with. She could twist it around, turn to her advantage. There was nothing she could do with this cold, emotionless demeanor.

"I do."

"You are dismissed."

Laureen returned to her room. Her bags were already packed. This would not end well for her. The queen did not take kindly to failure. She would not like losing a spy in the palace, not when replacing her now would be so difficult. She could only pray the information she had to give her would be enough to earn her forgiveness.

"Help me," a weak voice called from the darkness of the alley.

A young girl walking past stopped and looked for the person who spoke. "Hello?" she asked.

"Help me," the voice called again. Like an idiot, the girl walked into the darkness. Kern shook his head. You wouldn't see a Suriaxian falling for a trick like that. Alerians were much more trusting than he was accustomed to and easy prey for streetwise Suriaxians. He looked around, but there was no guard in sight. Coming up on the alley, he peered into the shadows. A man's hand was clamped firmly around the girl's mouth. She tried to fight her way loose, but he was larger and stronger. His other hand let go just long enough to conjure flames, effectively ending her resistance. Fear shone in her eyes.

"Hey, got mine." Another man walked up from the back of the alley and tossed down a woman bound in rope. She was half unconscious and had burns on her arms. "Nice," he leered at the girl the first man held. The girl shuddered. "Mind if I have a go?"

"This one's mine," the man answered. "At least until I'm done with her. Then I don't care what you do with her."

Kern assessed the situation. There were two targets, one standing alone and one holding a potential hostage. The latter would need to go first. There wasn't enough cover between them for him to sneak up unseen. Picking up a medium sized rock he took aim and hummed it at the man's head. He went out like a torch. Instead of running away as he hoped, the girl tripped over the man's prone body and fell to the ground. Kern ducked to avoid a fireball shot past his head. Thanks to this new Suriaxian gift, he would have to treat all his fights like he was facing a mage … who could throw a punch, he amended when the man followed up the fireball with his fist. Kern reached for his blade and remembered belatedly it was peace knotted. Alerian law specified all blades over twelve inches must be secured to one's person to avoid ease of access. The few seconds he spent reaching for a blade he could not draw found him on the ground nursing a sore jaw.

The man took out his own unsecured sword and took a swing at Kern. Kern jumped out of the way and pulled out a small utility kukri he kept for just such situations. Fighting a sword with a kukri was not ideal, but it gave him a weapon, and until he could loose his own sword, it was his only good option. He danced around the longer blade, attempting to find an opening he could exploit. The blade came down. Kern blocked with the kukri, grabbing the man's arm to dissipate some of the force, and pushed back, slashing across his abdomen. The man pulled back and grabbed his side. With rage in his eyes he ran at Kern, his sword coming down with enough force to cleave a man in two. Kern dodged and struck out with the kukri. A thin ribbon of red blossomed into a dripping waterfall of blood on the man's throat. He reached up to stop the bleeding, dropping his sword in the process, but it was too late. The man was dead before he hit the ground.

Kern took a couple of deep breaths and pulled out a rag to wipe the blood from his blade. That could have gone better, but he was alive, and the two women were alive and unmolested. He looked to the young girl and paused. She stared, unblinking, at the man's dead body. He recognized her expression as one of shock and horror. Her eyes followed the gathering pool of blood. "It's okay," he tried to comfort her. "He can't hurt you, now." She pulled back from his outstretched hand and sat hugging herself, shaking.

The other man moaned, eliciting a shriek from the girl. Kern kicked him back to sleep and continued to watch the girl, baffled by her reaction. It was as though she had never seen a dead body before. Then it hit him. They were in Aleria. It was entirely possible this was the first dead body she ever saw.

Kern tried to remember the first dead body he saw. It was difficult to sort through them all. The early days of Suriax were bloody, people going wild with the freedom to kill before retribution killings brought everything back down to more moderate levels. Frex tried to protect him at first, but that was quickly revealed as impossible. He remembered being fascinated. One minute a man could be walking down the street. The next he was dead, being carried away to bury or burn. He tried to remember how he felt, but he was far removed from that innocent boy.

"Put down the weapon."

Kern stifled a groan and complied. A soldier dressed in Alerian colors walked over carefully, looking at the two men on the ground and the two injured and frightened women. Other soldiers followed and began tending to the women. He thought they would arrest him, especially when they learned he was Suriaxian, but the girl, through a series of disjointed sentences and incoherent mumbles, filled them in on what had happened. And once the other woman was healed enough to talk, she confirmed what she could. Thanking him for his help but still looking at him with a fair amount of distrust, they let him go. He considered continuing his patrol, but the way the guards watched him leave killed that idea. If he stayed out, they would be watching him as much as anyone else. He would be a distraction, not a help. Feeling more lost than ever, he returned to the palace.

Lynnalin groaned and tried to move. Everything was dark. A massive weight on her chest made it difficult to breath. She coughed, but even that was painful. "There's someone over here," she heard a voice say over the ringing in her ears. The weight shifted, and an elf and two dwarves were lifting something large off her. She blinked against the light and blood in her eyes. She realized belatedly the elven man was talking to her, but she couldn't focus on his words. He helped her sit up and pressed a glass of water to her lips. "How are you feeling?" the man she finally recognized as the fighter Zanden asked.

Before she could respond, he was called over to the opposite side of the room. One of the dwarves held on to an adolescent marenpaie hound barking at a pile of rubble. Several men grabbed a side of one of the larger pieces and lifted, but the movement sent other pieces shifting. A man screamed in panic. "Don't, it's falling."

Lynnalin pushed herself up and hobbled over, making her way through the crowd. People were yelling suggestions of what to do. No one paid her much attention. Gathering her focus, she reached out a hand. "Leviedine." The rubble lifted into the air. While the others pulled the man out, she looked around. They were in the lobby of the stadium, but it was barely recognizable as such. Small fires burned. The spiral staircase that led to the balconies was broken in two spots, the gaps charred black. Pieces of the ceiling were missing. She could see smoke and shadows on the levels above. Distant voices and screams of pain confirmed the other rooms and sections of the building were in similar shape. Purses and other personal effects were left abandoned on the floor, coins and jewelry ignored as people walked over them to get to the bleeding and dying. Bodies were everywhere. She wondered where all the healers were. From the rays of sunlight pouring in through the front door she could see it was day, which meant many hours had passed since the fire rained from the sky last night. She walked to the door and saw why the clerics weren't there. The chaos was not restricted to the stadium. Destruction reined as far as she could see. Charred remains littered the ground. Bodies of those unfortunate enough to get caught in the stampede of those leaving the stadium were crushed, piled two high in some spots in a path from the building. A pool of blood five feet wide by ten feet long gathered at the foot of the steps. The sky was gray with smoke. Ash filled the air, blown around with every stray breeze.

'"Do you have any healing potions?" one of the dwarves asked.

Lynnalin reached absentmindedly into her pocket and pulled back sharply, her hand covered in blood. "Damn, I did, but they all broke." Carefully, she picked out a shard of glass from one of her cuts. The dwarf nodded and returned to his work.

"Hey, can you do that levitation spell again?" Zanden asked.

"Sure," Lynnalin turned from the door and joined the others, helping them free people the hound sniffed out of the rubble.

"Ok," one of the dwarves said. "This next one is going to be a little tricky." The stadium tree had many interior rooms on the first level. While most of the rooms on the upper levels had some kind of balcony access, there were quite a few first level rooms with only one entry point. One such room opened to the lobby and was currently blocked by the missing portions of the staircase and some other debris. A flash of light shone through the cracks. "Hey, kid," the dwarf yelled. "I already told you to cut it out with the fire. We're going to get you out of there." He turned and spoke to them. "Stupid kid is going to make the whole room collapse around him if he doesn't stop. And he better not have melted any of the money or burnt any of the bet vouchers, or I'll rip off his head and feed it to the hounds," he grumbled.

She must have made a face, because the other dwarf looked at her and chuckled. "Don't mind my brother. He's just upset because half the people who bet on the fights last night either ran or got killed."

"Ten years," he muttered. "It'll be another ten years before I can make back all those bets."

"My name is Rand," he continued while his brother ranted. "That's my brother, Larn."

"Lynnalin," she shook his hand. With her spells and their brawn, it didn't take long to make an opening they could use. Larn was the first to go in.

He disappeared into the darkness. All was quiet at first. Then he gave a curse and a fireball came flying out the door. She dodged to the side and lost her footing, falling over a twisted tree root in the floor. Larn came out carrying the boy by the back of his shirt. He dropped him unceremoniously on the floor. "Will you calm down already before you burn us all to ashes? You nearly caught my beard on fire."

"I'm sorry, I'm sorry, I'm sorry …" the boy blubbered. "I can't control it." His eyes widened in panic as his hands erupted in fire. He began waving them frantically, throwing off another fireball in the process.

Lynnalin looked down at her own hands. She remembered people being struck down by blue fire from the sky the previous night. She remembered trying to find a way out of the stadium. Everything was a little cloudy after that. "We can all do it," Zanden confirmed. "Or at least, all Suriaxians. Tourists weren't affected." He motioned over to a group of people huddling by a wall. The women were crying and shaking. The men stared forward with blank, haunted expressions.

"What happened?" She stood and dusted off her pants.

"No one knows," Rand answered. "The prevailing theory is that someone made a bargain with Venerith."

"Well," Larn interrupted, "We've done about as much as we can here. Let's move on to the next level. There are still plenty of people trapped and hiding."

"Are things this bad everywhere in the city?" Lynnalin asked.

"For the most part," Rand confirmed. "I went out earlier to get the hound to sniff out people in the rubble. It took me the entire morning to get to the stables and back." That was twice the time it should have taken. The stables were a fair distance away, but they were a relatively straight shot.

She looked at the sun dropping in the sky and did some quick calculations. "I have to go. I have some friends I want to check on, and I'll need to leave now if I hope to make it before dark."

Rand handed the hound's leash to his brother. "I'll go with you."

"That isn't necessary."

"You haven't seen what it's like out there."

"I can take care of myself," she argued."

"Look, you're fourth decade, right?" he asked, indicating her burgundy cloak, standard issue for students entering their final decade of study.

Lynnalin nodded. A mage in Suriax went through twenty years of basic magic classes followed by another thirty years of advanced studies. Suriaxians took their education seriously. All children were sent to early learning academies at the age of fifteen. It was there they were administered a series of aptitude tests to determine their ideal placement in specialized academies. Of course the ultimate choice of which school to attend was left up to the families. Suriaxians were strong believers in a person's ability to succeed out of sheer willpower and would never underestimate someone who chose to attempt a vocation the tests showed a low aptitude for. Because of this focus on willpower and a drive to succeed, their schools were some of the best on the entire continent. Everyone knew it and praised Suriax for its skilled craftsmen, but you would not find many from outside the city in attendance. Suriaxians were highly competitive and ruthless. It was not uncommon for the top ranks of the class to not live to graduation. Eliminating the competition was something all Suriaxians excelled at. Although cheating was a punishable offense, it was more out of an effort to teach the students the benefits of not getting caught than out of any moral imperative. In Suriax you were taught it was not enough to be smart. You must also survive. A wise student learned to sit somewhere just behind the leaders instead of sticking out as the best. Lynnalin was fifth in her class.

"Have you ever been in a war?" She shook her head. "Well, that's what it's like out there. It's a war zone. Imagine a class full of first year mage students given access to your kind of power." She shuddered. "Exactly."

Now she was even more worried about Bryce and Marcy. While Suriaxians could be ruthless and heartless in the pursuit of their goals, they were fiercely loyal to those they called friends. Lynnalin headed for the door, Rand behind her. The smells of death and decay were stronger now that the corpses had been lying in the sun all day. Men clothed in cloaks with collars made of feathers and masks in the shape of birds, huddled in small groups over the bodies. They wore armor and jewelry made of bones and their legs were bound by strips of leather, invoking the appearance of bird legs. While most of their bone apparel was clean and white, there were a few sporting newer bones still covered in bits of bloody flesh. Silently, they ripped off pieces of meat from the bodies, eating it raw. Almost as one they looked up at her as she approached, but after a few jerky head movements eerily reminiscent of the avians they dressed as, they paid her no further attention. Holding her cloak up and to the side, she slid down the banister to the ground. Rand walked down the steps, pushing bodies out of his way with his foot. He gave the bird men a wide berth. "Damned birds give me the creeps," he muttered once they were out of earshot.

Lynnalin nodded her agreement. The men were clerics of the bird god Ferogid. He was a god of pestilence and undeath. His followers wore bone armor to mimic his emaciated vulture/humanoid form. They had a sixth sense about death and were drawn to battles and disasters. While it was not uncommon to see them picking through the remains of the recently deceased, eating the raw flesh from the bones, it was said they took older corpses back to their temples to perform rituals to raise the poor souls, creating undead servants for their god. That was one reason the citizens of Suriax were so inclined to follow the rules regarding killing in the city. Suriax had an agreement with the temple of Ferogid that allowed them access to anyone killed in the city. As long as all the appropriate papers were filed, bodies were turned over right away with the assurance they would not be raised. Anyone else was given over without such assurances.

The ground was littered with streamers, confetti, jewelry and coins, covered in grime and submerged in random puddles. A woman carried buckets of water, pouring them out on two fires blazing in a small home. Her face was red and blistered with fresh burns. She watched suspiciously as Lynnalin and Rand walk by. Her reaction was not unusual. Those who saw them either ran in fear or looked at them as though they were the cause of their misfortune. The only exception was a group of laughing men who leered at her suggestively. One took a step toward her, but Rand tapped his hammer against his hand threateningly. The men ducked back inside the building where they stood. Lynnalin pulled up her hood and kept walking.

A noise beginning as a soft din in the distance grew to a

yelling mob. Dozens of people surrounded a small store. Glass broke and men jumped through the front window, climbing on other people already inside. Someone ran out with a barrel of mead and was tackled by a man on the street. The barrel fell and broke, its contents spilling on the street. The second man cursed and shot fire at the first man, roasting him on the spot. He turned and pushed his way back in the store. Light flared inside, quickly turning into a raging fire. The crowd surged, emptying onto the street in a wave. Lynnalin was caught without a way to get out. All around people pressed into her, stepping on her feet, elbows digging into her back and chest, hair in her face. She couldn't see the street. She couldn't see where her arms were. Someone pulled on her cloak, choking her in the process. She reached up and grabbed the tie, trying to get her fingers between the fabric and her throat. Hands groped her breasts. At some point she realized her feet were no longer touching the ground. Hands on her back lifted her up and carried her deeper into the crowd. Even with her fingers trying desperately to pull at her cloak, she felt her vision blur.

Then the pressure was gone. She took in several gasping breaths, noticing later she was sitting on the ground. She could see the ground again for a few feet in every direction. A flaming hammer swung over her head. Rand reached down and helped her to her feet. Holding out his hammer, he led them through the crowd. She saw several bodies with heads bashed in littering the ground. Once they were clear, he let the fire go out. Fresh blood covered the side of his hammer. Already forgetting her and Rand, the crowd attacked the next store across the street. "Thank you." Rand grunted in response, eyes trained on their surroundings for potential threats. They walked in silence until they were well past the courthouse. Rounding the corner, she could see the Arrow's Quill in the distance. Picking up her pace, she rushed there. People ransacked a few businesses down the street, but for the moment the tavern was quiet. The scorched bodies just outside the door suggested Bryce had worked hard to get it that way. "Stand back," she warned Rand before opening the door. If she knew Bryce, he would be jumpy right about now. The fire ball that came at her the moment the door was open proved her caution valid. "Stinguest," she said. The flame extinguished before it could reach her. "Bryce, it's me," she called.

"Lynnalin? I'm sorry." She took a look around and cringed. There were scorch marks everywhere. The curtains were in tatters on the floor. "Come on in. Have a drink." He poured two drinks and pushed them forward.

"This is Rand," she introduced. "Rand, meet Bryce." They nodded their greetings. "Where's Marcy?" Bryce's eyes grew hooded. "She left town. I don't know where she is, now."

"What do mean? I just saw her the other day. She didn't say anything about leaving town."

"It had something to do with Kern. There were Royal Guards staking the place out for days looking for him. They wanted her to lead them to him."

"That's why she wanted the scroll," she realized.

Rand finished his drink and set down his mug. "Well," he said, standing, "I should get back to the stadium. Thanks for the drink." He opened the door to leave and nearly fell over from the weight people trying to get in the tavern. Pushing against three men, he struggled with the door. Bryce ran over and put his body weight into pushing the door closed. Hands reached around Rand. People were yelling to be allowed in. Some wanted food. Some wanted to drink. Some wanted to plunder the building for any and all valuables.

"Somniedus," Lynnalin commanded. The men at the door fell asleep. Without their weight against the door, it slammed shut. After taking a moment to get over their surprise, Rand and Bryce barred the door.

"Are you alright?" Bryce asked.

She tried to stop the spinning in her head. Her head injury was beginning to throb, not that the pain bothered her, but it did make concentration difficult. Add to that a less than restful night unconscious, and she was near her limits for spell casting for the time being. She needed a good night's sleep. "I will be, but we need to figure out a long term solution. Those people won't stay asleep forever, and there are even more the spell didn't reach. It isn't safe here."

Bryce looked around the tavern. "I know," he said dejectedly. He had built this business from nothing. The idea of leaving it to be destroyed was not easy to swallow. Before they could discuss options, the window erupted into a fiery spray of glass and wood. A stone planter rolled through the room, coming to rest by Lynnalin. Fire shot through the opening, catching her cloak on fire. "Stinguest," she said quickly. The flames went out, but not before leaving a hole big enough to stick her fingers through.

"Open up or I'll throw in another fireball," someone called from the street.

"Fireball?" Lynnalin asked. Gathering her cloak she stormed to the window, climbing up on a table and out the opening. The street full of men and women stopped their fighting to look up at her. Well, *her* and the large ball of fire growing between her hands. "You call that a fireball?" The flame that was a bright glowing red turned to blue and white as she fed in her own fire. The flames flared out, engulfing everyone for fifty feet. Anyone caught in the blast disintegrated into ash. She looked out at those left. "This tavern is off limits. Now go find someplace else to loot." She waited for the street to clear before going back inside. Jumping down from the table, she headed to the back where Bryce kept his spare bed. "Let me know if they come back."

"Where are you going?" Rand asked.

"To sleep."

"Can we talk?" Eirae sat down next to Kern, their backs to one of the many balcony gardens in the palace. His eyes and tone suggested a serious conversation.

"It was self-defense," Kern started without preamble. "He attacked me." This was ridiculous. All he wanted to do was help some people, and now he was being judged for killing that man. What kind of backwards place was this anyway? He was starting to miss Suriax. At least things made sense there.

"I'm not here to discuss what happened today. No one faults you for your actions. We all know you saved those two women's lives."

"Then what do you want to talk about?" he asked, mollified, but confused.

Eirae collected his thoughts and continued. "I want to talk about your feelings on killing."

Kern groaned "What is this, an intervention? Let me guess, you want to talk to me about the error of my ways and how killing is evil?"

Eirae laughed. "So, Pielere got to you first, then," he said to himself. "I guess we can't help wanting to meddle. We are accustomed to making decisions that affect the lives of thousands of people, and we take family obligations seriously. As such, Pielere and I are prone to unsolicited advice. Just ask Mirerien."

He scrunched his face. He was annoyed at having his life scrutinized, his life choices questioned, but it was somewhat comforting to be called family. "Honestly I didn't expect you three to believe me so easily, much less take to giving brotherly advice."

"Mirerien believed you. She's never wrong about that sort of thing. She has a knack for knowing if someone is telling the truth."

"Really?" he asked, intrigued. "So what's your special power?"

"What do you mean?"

"Well, Mirerien knows if someone is lying. Pielere can hear voices of people asking for help."

"Pielere hears voices? That explains a lot." he shook his head. "We're getting off topic."

"Look, yes I'm with the Flame Guard. Yes, I've killed people. I'm surprised you have a problem with that. After all, you're known as the Punisher. Are you telling me you've never sentenced someone to die?"

"There is a difference between having someone executed for a crime and going out and killing someone because you want to."

"I never just killed people because I wanted to or because I enjoyed it. It was my job, and it was all legal." He found himself returning to that argument, almost as a desperate last attempt to justify his actions. He had never questioned the moral choice to take a life before. It was not something anyone in Suriax thought of or talked about. Killing happened. Death was something you grew accustomed to. Now, he wasn't so sure. He never felt guilty about his life before, not even when his uncle criticized him about it, but now … now he found he did not want them to think poorly of him. He didn't want his new family to be disappointed in who their brother was. It was stupid. He didn't even know them, but they accepted him, and a part of him didn't want to lose that.

Sensing the conflict in Kern, Eirae's tone softened. "I don't have a problem with killing if it is justified. If someone commits a crime, there needs to be a consequence. That is what keeps society moving, what keeps order. The fear of punishment is what keeps people from breaking the law. While it may be legal to kill in Suriax, that doesn't make it justified. That is where our father lost his way. He became distracted with what was legal, with what he could get away with, and stopped being a steward of the law. You say you killed on orders. What were the crimes of the people you were sent to kill?"

Kern thought back. Many of the people he killed were not

pleasant individuals; they were killers, thieves, all around cruel people, but there were some who were guilty of no crimes. He was sent to kill people who challenged the queen's authority, people who spoke out against her or annoyed her. He had never questioned that before coming here.

Eirae put a hand on Kern's arm. "Just think about it."

Kern felt his head spin. His vision blurred for a second. "Okay," he mumbled, before heading back to his room. Suddenly, he felt very tired. He turned the corner down the hall and came up short. Marcy and Thomas were standing at the door of her room. Thomas looked down at her, stroking her face affectionately. His head lowered, their lips were about to meet, when everything went black.

Kern awoke feeling groggy. He rubbed his face and came instantly awake. His hands were sticky and smelled of blood. A quick glance confirmed the smell. He patted his body but did not find any injuries. Dried blood stained his clothes and bed sheets. He saw he still wore his day clothes, including his boots. Trying to remember when he came to bed and whose blood he was covered in, he looked around the room for clues. Everything looked untouched. He saw no sign of a struggle, no dead body, nothing to tell him what happened.

The door flew open. "Murderer!" Thomas came running in. Guards held him back, but he continued to scream at Kern. "You killed her," he accused.

"Who?" Kern asked.

Two guards grabbed his arms and pulled him off the bed. "Kern Tygierrenon, you are under arrest for the murder of Marcy Kentalee."

Kern looked around his small cell. The walls were stone. They normally housed criminals in the prison, crafted from magic from a large tree, but given his ability to create fire they were taking special precautions. Truth be told, he hadn't gotten the hang of calling the fire yet. He was just as likely to kill himself as to escape. But they weren't taking any chances. The room was empty, not even a cot or chair. He sat on the cold stone floor and stared at his hands. The blood was dry now. He still couldn't believe it. Marcy was dead. He'd never hear her laugh again. He would never see her smile. And they thought he was responsible. He could never kill Marcy. He loved her. Yes, he was jealous of the way she looked at Thomas, but what sense would it make to kill her? Of course, no one listened to him. He was covered in her blood. Even he knew that was suspicious. He had no idea where the blood came from.

The door opened. He squinted against the bright sunlight. Once his eyes adjusted, he saw his uncle standing there. The look of disappointment cut through him. "How could you?" Frex's voice broke.

"Uncle, I didn't ," Kern pleaded.

"Do not tell me lies. I knew … I knew what you were becoming, and I didn't stop you. Her death is as much my fault as yours. I should have stopped you. I failed your mother. I failed you. For that, I am sorry." He turned to go. "I can't do this anymore. This is the last time we will speak. Goodbye, Kern."

"No!" Kern raced to the door but the guard slammed it in his face, and for the first time since his mother died, Kern cried.

How much time passed, he did not know. The only light in the cell came from a small lantern near the ceiling. No one else visited him, not that he expected them to. If Frex believed him guilty and never wanted to see him again, he could only imagine the reaction he would get from his siblings. They hardly even knew him. They had no reason to believe in his innocence. Still, when he was finally led from the room and brought to the courts before them, he felt the last of his hope die. Pielere and Mirerien couldn't even look him in the eye. That was still better than Eirae, who looked at him with unveiled contempt. He argued again that it was a mistake, but no one was listening.

After a while he stopped arguing and sat in stunned silence. He didn't resist when they led him back to the cell. They would most likely have him executed. That didn't bother him so much. He had killed enough people over the years that it was probably justified. What did bother him was the thought of Marcy's killer on the loose. Who would want to kill her? Why set him up for it? Would they go after other people he cared for? Maybe bringing his uncle here hadn't protected him at all. Maybe it put him in greater danger. There were too many unknowns.

The door opened, someone entered the cell, but he didn't bother looking up, expecting it was someone dropping off food. He couldn't remember the last time he ate, not that he had any appetite. It occurred to him the only person who would want to hurt him who had the connections to plan something like this was Maerishka. She probably wanted to ruin his reputation so that, should he try to take the throne from her, he would not receive any support from Aleria.

Kern looked up and saw he was wrong about the identity of his visitor. Mirerien stood by the door. Her eyes squinted in distress. Without a word, she turned to leave.

"Wait!" He stood, his legs unsteady from hours of sitting. "I didn't kill her, and you know it. You must let me out."

"I cannot circumvent the law based on a feeling." Her eyes burned through him.

"So instead you let an innocent man be convicted of a crime he didn't commit?"

"Can you tell me how you came to have her blood on you or how your blade was used to stab her repeatedly?"

Kern cringed. The description of Marcy's death was painful to hear. Her attack spoke of rage, lending credence to the theory Kern killed her out of jealousy. "I'm being set up," he answered weakly.

Mirerien's eyes softened. "I know."

Nothing left to say, she left. He didn't know what he expected her to do. He was on his own.

CHAPTER SEVEN

KERN WAITED, A PLAN BEGINNING TO FORM. HE NEEDED TO FIND the person responsible for Marcy's death and clear his name. Practicing with calling his fire, he sat by the door of his cell. They brought him food twice a day, so all he had to do was time things right. Humming a song to keep himself awake, he still fought against sleep. It wasn't that he was all that tired, but squatting by the door, poised to strike, staring at a plain stone wall, took its toll. When he finally heard the door knob turn, it startled him out of a half sleep. He almost burned the guard by accident, barely missing as he shot fire past the guard's leg. The man jumped back reflexively and Kern pushed the door into him, knocking the man over and buying himself a few seconds to run past him. Ducking into a side hall, he heard the man call out for help. Other guards ran past his hiding place. Grabbing a lone guard, he knocked the man unconscious and took his coat and hat. Then he rushed down another hall, blending in to the chaos surrounding his jailbreak. He kept a low profile, making his way through the city. By nightfall he reached the southern gates.

Kern looked down the long bridge home. He had never thought he would return to Suriax, yet here he was. Still posing as a guard, he easily slipped past the gate. Ditching the uniform in the crowd, he took in the chaos around him. The few riots that had sprung up in Aleria were nothing compared to what he found in Suriax. People were fighting, some out of anger, some for fun. Fire shot out through the air at every turn. Buildings burned, people screamed. Getting to the palace without being stopped was easy. He grabbed an extra change of clothes from home so he could be recognized as one of the Flame Guard. Looking at Frex's chair and clothes threatened to break his self-control. He steeled himself against the pain of Frex's disappointment and pushed on. He didn't have time to feel bad for himself. Once he cleared his name, hopefully things would go back to the way they were between them.

It didn't take him long to find Maerishka. She was always in the gardens this time of day. He saw her seated by a fountain talking to a robed man. The man's cowl shifted and Kern felt himself go numb. It was Cornerbluff. He was alive. They laughed, Maerishka asking about his mission. He described, in horrific detail, murdering Marcy and framing Kern. "It was simple," he boasted. "I posed as a servant and put a sleep potion in his drink. He didn't wake until the next morning when the body was found. He was still covered in the blood I poured on him. When I left, they had him on trial for her murder. He may even have been executed already. You won't have to worry about Kern Tygierrenon again."

"Excellent." Maerishka stood and handed him a small leather sack. It landed in his hands with a jingle, coins falling from the loose opening in the top. "Worth every silver."

She left Cornerbluff to count his rewards. So distracted was he, he did not see Kern approach until he was only a few inches away. Cornerbluff jumped. Coins dropped to the ground, rolling out of sight.

"Remember me?" he backed away a few steps. "I remember you. I remember killing you. Guess once wasn't enough. Should I try again?"

"Wait, I was just following orders. It wasn't personal."

"Wasn't personal? You killed a woman. What did she ever do to you? She was innocent. If you had a problem with me, come after me."

"I was following orders," he said again.

"Orders? Orders?" Kern let his anger rise. "She wasn't orders. She was a person. She had a name, a life, a family. You took all that away." Cornerbluff backed away from Kern's tirade, but he kept pressing forward. "You killed her. Maerishka may have ordered it, but you are the one who took her life. You are the one who savagely stabbed her and took her away from those who love her. You could have said 'no,' but you didn't. You could have said 'no.'"

Cornerbluff bumped into a column and stopped, nowhere else to go. He looked around frantically. "I didn't do anything wrong. Espionage killing in Aleria for the queen is only illegal if you get caught."

"But it was wrong," Kern thundered. At the look of complete bafflement from the old half gnome, Kern stopped. A week earlier, their roles could have been reversed. Was this what he sounded like justifying his actions to Eirae and Pielere? He felt bile rise in his throat at the thought. Disgusted, he walked off. Cornerbluff shifted his weight in confusion. "You aren't going to kill me?"

Kern stopped and considered. "No, it wouldn't do any good. She's dead. Killing you won't bring her back. But if you or Maerishka ever come after someone I care about again, I will track you both down and show you the same mercy you showed Marcy."

Walking away, he felt lightheaded. Dizziness sent him spinning. He fell to his knees to avoid hurting himself should he lose consciousness.

"Are you okay?" a woman asked.

Kern looked up, his vision clearing, and saw Marcy kneeling beside him. He stood and took a step back. His clothes were changed back to what he wore in Aleria the day she died, but they were not stained with blood. His surroundings had changed as well. No longer standing in Maerishka's garden, instead he stood in the hallway leading to his room in the Alerian palace. Marcy looked at him with concern, clearly worried by his strange behavior, but unsure what to say. Thomas stood behind. It was then he remembered where he was. "I'm fine. I just need to rest." Unable to stop staring at her, afraid she would disappear should he look away, he backed up several more steps before finally turning to go. Thomas followed after, pulling Kern aside.

"Is this about what you saw just now? I've been wanting to talk to you about Marcy. I know we never discussed what she is to you, and I don't want to step on your toes. It just sort of happened," Thomas rambled on guiltily.

It took a moment to remember what he was referring to, his mind still partially lost in that weird dream world. "It's fine. Whatever feelings I may have had for her don't matter. We were only ever friends." At one time, he may have been angry or jealous. Now he was just relieved she lived.

"Are you sure?" Thomas' eyes beamed with relief. He obviously cared a great deal for her and would cherish her. She deserved that.

"Yes."

Thomas smiled and left Kern alone with his thoughts. What was that weird dream? It felt incredibly real. He still felt the weight of his chains and could still smell the blood on his clothes. Maybe it was a side effect of the blue fire, or maybe his head injury was more severe than he thought.

"Eirae," Mirerien called.

"Over here," Eirae answered from his seat by the garden, a small book in his hand. He still sat where Kern left him, as though he was waiting for something. Putting the book away, he stood and greeted his sister.

"I require your assistance. There is a young man accused of

setting fire to a building. Thankfully no one died, but there were injuries. I know he is lying about not being there, but I cannot get him to admit what part he played in the fire. He is being very non-cooperative. Could you use your persuasion to get to the truth?"

"Of course."

"Bring him," she called. The guards led a young half elf boy to stand before them. The boy shook but stood defiantly tall.

Eirae put a hand on his shoulder and spoke with a hauntingly soft voice. "We need to know what happened so we can prevent further injury."

The boy swayed, his eyes glassing over. Then he snapped to full attention and looked around in a panic. "What am I … what is going on? How am I back here?"

"How did the fire start?" Eirae asked without acknowledging his questions.

The boy looked away with a mixture of guilt and pain. "It was my girlfriend. She is Suriaxian. I just wanted to see the fire. She said she could control it, but she couldn't put it out." His eyes were haunted. "She didn't want to hurt anyone."

Kern felt his jaw go slack. He waited for Eirae and Mirerien to be alone and stepped into the sunlight. "You did the same thing to me that you did to him. You messed with my head, gave me that nightmare."

"Nightmare?" Mirerien asked. "What did you do?" She eyed Eirae with reproach.

"I only planted a suggestion. Your conscience did the rest," he said to Kern. "If you had no guilt, it would not have worked."

"Why would you want to do that?"

"Look, no offense, but we don't know you," he answered matter-of-factly. "And we've been burned by family before. I'm not about to let it happen again. I had to be sure we could trust you."

That made some sense, but he still did not like the idea of

being manipulated. "And what, you can just make people see whatever you want?"

"Not exactly. Your mind came up with your torture. You had your own doubts. I just made you face them."

"Eirae!" Mirerien admonished. "He is our brother, not some criminal." He shrugged.

"How?" He could worry about the why or being angry with his brother later. Right now, he wanted to understand how something like this was even possible.

"Don't know. I realized I could do it while interrogating prisoners. It's a very effective means of getting confessions." His eyes gleamed with smug satisfaction.

"What are you people? How can you do these things? This isn't normal. Normal people don't manipulate dreams or hear strangers' prayers, or act as some truth detector."

"Hear prayers?" Mirerien asked.

"Pielere," Eirae explained.

"Ah," she said, understanding.

"This is what I'm talking about. You aren't even surprised."

They shared a look. "We have felt different for some time," Mirerien said. "As our names grew, and more people began to ask for our help in settling disputes, we each noticed changes; slowed aging, a boost in energy after celebrations in our name. We don't understand the cause, but we ceased to be surprised by these anomalies long ago."

"And we would prefer if they did not become common knowledge," Eirae added, pointedly.

Kern bristled. "You think I'm going to go around revealing your secrets?"

"I return to my earlier comment. We don't know you."

Mirerien put a hand on Eirae's arm and shot him a look. "Do you promise not to tell anyone?"

Kern almost answered automatically that he would not. Then he saw the intense way she stared at him and realized she was using her truth telling ability to see if he would lie to them.

"Trust me or don't. I don't care. If you are so paranoid that you can't trust anyone without cheating, then I feel sorry for you." She had the decency to look away guiltily. "I think my being here is a mistake. I'm thankful our uncle has a safe place to stay, but that little nightmare of yours pointed out a loose end I need to take care of if I want him to stay safe." Not waiting for a reply, he left.

Elisteen pulled out a loaf of bread and smiled with satisfaction. It was a perfect golden brown. She checked the rolls and started the next batch of dough. This job wasn't as easy as it had been when she was younger, but she still enjoyed the work, and she enjoyed creating a good product people could appreciate. She wiped her brow and stopped in shock. Standing on the other side of the counter was King Pielere. He smiled warmly and wished her a good morning. She stumbled over a greeting. One of the three Alerian monarchs stood in her little bakery. No one would believe it. She didn't believe it. "What can I get you, Your Majesty?"

"What do you recommend?"

"The sweet rolls are a specialty of mine," she beamed proudly, handing him several on a plate. "Here, on the house."

He thanked her and sat at one of the tables. Elisteen pretended to clean, all the while watching him from the corner of her eye. He ate slowly with all the refinement of a royal, not dripping any glaze or spilling any crumbs. She almost jumped out of her skin when the back door opened. "Alnerand, what are you doing here? You should be resting."

"I'm fine." He pulled out an apron and put it on with a grimace. "I can help you." He attempted to tie the apron and gave up, holding on to his arm.

She pushed up his sleeve to reveal an array of purple, blue and black bruises. Holding on to his arm tight enough to make him flinch, and thus prove her point, she berated him. "This is not fine. You are lucky you can even use this arm right now. If that horse had kicked any harder, it would have broken the bone."

"I'm okay, Grandma." He put his other hand over hers and smiled reassuringly.

"Is that so?" another voice said. Their landlord, Grieland, and his entourage walked up to the counter. Casually on purpose, they knocked over her plants. The glass vases broke into many small shards and soil spilled out on the floor. Laughing, they grabbed some bread out of the display case on the counter and made a point out of eating it in front of her. "In that case, you should have shown up for your work this morning."

"I am at work," Alnerand responded, angrily. As a point, he reached around, ignoring the pain, and tied his apron in place."

"Oh, I don't think so. You owe me fifty silver for that wagon you broke yesterday."

"Your horse kicked me into that wagon."

"Maybe you should have done a better job shoeing him."

"I'm not a farrier or a blacksmith. I'm a baker."

"You are what I say you are if you want your grandmother to keep her home."

"Is this how you normally treat your tenants?" the king asked, speaking at last.

"Mind your own business," Grieland replied without looking back. Chair legs scraped against the floor, and the tone in the room shifted as everyone else saw who was in the room. Sensing the change, Grieland turned and backed up against the counter. "I'm sorry. I didn't mean … I didn't know it was you."

Pielere walked toward the group. All the others parted immediately, eyes darting to the door as they considered making an escape. "Perhaps it is time your permits and licenses came under review. As I know you are aware, we have strong ethics codes that pertain to all business conducted in the city.

Violation of these codes can be a very serious offense." Grieland didn't speak, too afraid to move. "Now, I believe you were about to pay the lady for the food your group has eaten and the damage you and your friends have done."

"Of course, Your Majesty." Shaking, he pulled out a coin purse and removed a handful of silver. Pielere raised an eyebrow and he quickly added a few gold pieces. "Excellent. Someone will be visiting you within the week to go over your business dealings and conduct interviews. You may go." The lot of them bolted from the bakery. Alnerand laughed and hugged Elisteen. She felt tears in her eyes.

"Thank you, Your Majesty. You have no idea what this means to us."

Pielere inclined his head in response. "Contact the palace should you have any further problems with that man. Thank you for the sweet rolls. They were excellent." With that he left. Still in disbelief over what just happened, Elisteen went over to his table to clean and found a small bag sitting there. It was a simple brown bag with gold trim and a leather drawstring. Opening the bag, she found it full of coins.

"Grandmother, what is that?" Alnerand asked.

"A miracle," she answered. "A miracle."

Maerishka looked out her balcony at the city. The fires were mostly out. The initial chaos that had followed the night of blue fire was beginning to ebb. Already, people were beginning to master their new skills. She thought to herself it should make the Tournament of Fire interesting when it restarted in a month. She grinned. Her people were nothing if not adaptive. Of course it was little fun to burn someone who could burn you back. The fire was a great equalizer, making every citizen a dangerous weapon. Those wishing to exploit their new strength on those weaker had mostly crossed the border to Aleria. The Alerians were easy prey. She contemplated sending her troops across the border to wrest control of the city from her sniveling half siblings, but she knew better than to underestimate the strength of their military. Their lands were vast, and they could easily call reinforcements.

"Your Highness," Svanteese entered. Even he looked nervous to be around her now. While everyone was effected by the fire, none were as much so as she. Her body maintained an unnaturally high temperature no amount of healing spells could remedy. Her skin was hot to the touch and if she maintained physical contact for too long, she could burn another without calling forth the flames. Another useful side effect was she could not herself be burned, and her mastery of the flames far exceeded that of anyone else.

"Laureen is here to see you."

Maerishka hid her surprise. They had not spoken in person in almost ten years. Until now, they only communicated via magical means and couriered messages. Travel between the two cities was prohibited as it could lead to others learning of her identity. Travel across the border was not restricted but it was monitored, especially for palace staff and their families. "Let her in." The girl who entered looked meek and unassuming. Her clothes were simple servant's garb. Her hair was pulled back in a loose braid. Dirt smudged her face. It was all a lie. Laureen was a deadly warrior within the Flame Guard and one of her main spies stationed in Aleria.

"Why have you come here?"

"I'm afraid I will no longer be able to serve in my former capacity. Getting struck down with blue fire in the middle of a crowded room was a little difficult to explain. The palace now checks all guests and servants for the flame mark on our necks."

"I see."

"I did learn one thing that you may find useful." Laureen hastened to add.

"Go on."

"There was a member of the Flame Guard by the name of Kern Tygierrenon staying as a special guest at the palace. He broke in to the quarters of the queen, but instead of having him arrested, they gave him a room and servants to attend him. Word around the palace is that he is their brother."

Maerishka felt her eyes widen reflexively. This was her first confirmation his claim to her throne could be legitimate. If they allowed him to remain in the palace, they must believe him. "Anything else?"

The tone in her voice must have given something away, because Laureen instantly stiffened. "No, Your Highness."

"In that case," Maerishka walked forward and ran a finger casually across Laureen's arm. She sucked in a quick breath, clearly uncomfortable but attempting to hide her discomfort. "Your services will no longer be needed." Maerishka walked back to her desk and poured a drink.

Laureen gripped her arm, no longer trying to hide her pain. "What did you do to me?"

"That burning you feel in your arm will soon spread through your veins, into the rest of your body. Your blood is beginning to boil," she described. "You are cooking from the inside out. Don't worry," she said at the look of panic in her eyes. "It will be excruciating, but once the heat reaches your brain, you will go too crazy to know what is happening." After that, her only response was screams.

———

Kern felt déjà vu as he stared at the palace. There wasn't as much fighting in Suriax as he expected to find, but the destruction left over was evident. He grabbed his spare guardsman clothes, taking a moment to look around his onetime home. Seeing his uncle's chair brought back all the pain he felt in his dream. He shook it off, reminding himself it wasn't real. His uncle was safe and happy in Aleria. About to leave, he saw something green and blue beside the chair on the floor. He picked up his mother's scarf. The yarn was rough but warm. He thought back to the day she gave it to Frex. That was the last day either of them saw her alive. That was the last day either of them saw her, period, he amended. They weren't able to go to her funeral. He was never able to pay his respects. She sacrificed herself to keep him safe, to protect him from his father. What would she think of the man he became? Would she think it was all worth it? Feeling unusually retrospective, probably a side effect of whatever Eirae had done to him, Kern wrapped the scarf around his neck and tucked it under his coat. It was a little warm to be wearing a scarf, but he did not care. This was all he had of his mother, a woman he had never truly appreciated, and he wanted it close to him. Closing the door to his home, Kern left.

Maerishka stood at her balcony. The room still smelled of burnt flesh. Leaving the window open to let the smell out, she returned to her inner chamber and changed into a new gown for Lord Alvexton's departure. He was the only visiting dignitary to stay after the chaos of the night of fire. He was to return home briefly to see to some issues needing his attention, but he planned to return once the tournament resumed. She smiled. It appeared she was right to choose him as her paramour. So what if he didn't know he was chosen yet? It wasn't really his choice, anyway. She would get what she wanted, one way or another. And once he was under her thumb completely, she would have access to a great deal more land and resources. Yes, a union between them would be very beneficial to her.

The hair on her neck stood on end, a strange shiver running down her back. Looking around, she confirmed she was alone. Maerishka stepped back into the main room and paused. A flame guardsman stood by the window, leaning casually against the frame. "Hello, Sister."

"Kern Tygierrenon, I presume."

He inclined his head in confirmation. "I must say," Kern ran a hand along the curtain absentmindedly, "your palace is much easier to break into than our siblings' up north. You should probably have someone look into enhancing your security."

"I don't need security." Maerishka poured a drink, purposefully turning her back to him to appear unconcerned by his presence. She swallowed the drink and allowed it to fortify her and calm her unease. "You call me sister, but I do not know you?" She turned back to face him.

"I am your half-brother. My mother hid me from our father."

"I suppose you want to exploit our blood connection for some sort of high ranking political or military position. Or perhaps you just wish for money."

"No."

"No?"

"I want to be left alone. Call off your guards and leave me and my friends alone. If your desire was to keep our relationship secret it is too late."

"That changes nothing." She walked toward him and put her hand on his chest. Kern eyed her suspiciously. Through his jacket and scarf, he began to feel an immense heat. He jumped back and the heat dissipated. He could see the surprise in her eyes. "You do not burn?"

"Just special, I guess." Anger flared in her eyes.

"What do you want from me?" Kern dodged Maerishka's flame encircled fist.

"I want you to die." She reached for him and the fire flared out, burning the side of his face before he could move.

In response to the pain, his hands came alive with fire. Stepping back from another advance, he forced the fire to go out. Whatever else he was, he would not attack his own sister, even if she was trying to kill him, even if she had killed their father. He was not her. He wasn't the mindless killer his brothers thought him to be. Deciding further conversation was pointless at that moment he jumped off the balcony, swinging down on the rope he had left tied there. Maerishka jumped off the balcony, her fall slowing just before she reached the ground. Her feet touched down softly on the grass. It figured she'd have a slow descent spell enchanting something she wore. "Royals," he swore under his breath. Kern ducked as another flame shot over his head and stepped to the right, jumping over a small stone wall to put some distance between them. He needed a plan. The wall of the building in front of him went up in flames. He stopped and turned to face her. "I don't want your throne. I'm no threat to you."

She held her hands in front of her, ready to shoot another flame at him at any moment. "Maybe not now, but what is to stop you from changing your mind in a year or ten? I need to get rid of you now, before anyone else finds out you exist and uses it to undermine my authority. You have to die."

"You enjoy killing your family that much?"

The dig actually caught her off guard. Her hands lowered a fraction of an inch. "I killed our father and my mother in self-defense. They were going to have me murdered. Father believed I would betray him." She didn't know why she felt the need to defend her actions. She was always more than happy to let everyone else believe her a cold blooded, power hungry killer. But she cared for her parents at one time. Their betrayal struck her hard, killing what was left of her compassion. Of course she wasn't that surprised her father didn't trust her, but her mother was another matter. She thought they were close. Her mother taught her to fight, taught her how to lead. Her mother made her who she was, and in an instant it was all gone.

"I don't want your throne," he repeated softly. "I don't want to rule. I just want to be left alone."

She looked at him indecisively. "How can I possibly believe

AMANDA YOUNG & RAYMOND YOUNG JR.

you? Perhaps you are just buying time until you can master your fire ability."

"I don't know what else to say," he threw his hands up in frustration. It seemed none of his estranged siblings felt they could trust him. "I didn't even want this fire curse or blessing or whatever it was you called down on all of us. I just want to be me, not some ruler and not some pawn of a god I don't even believe in anymore. I want no part of Suriax or Venerith. I would give it all up and never look back. I swear that to you and to the universe. Do you hear that, Venerith?" he called up to the heavens. "I forsake you and your gifts." Pain surged through his body. His soul burned, and he thought he would finally die. He thought there was no one other than perhaps his uncle who would care. Maybe it was for the best. The back of his neck, where the flame mark could be found, flared hot enough to be felt over the other pain. Flames shot out of his pores, creating a funnel of heat and fire around him. His clothing burned, the edges coming off as ash, drifting away a few inches before disintegrating from the heat. In a violent rush that left him cold and without air, the flames shot up to the sky. As the pain subsided he found himself on his hands and knees, struggling to breathe.

Maerishka's face broke into a grin. She called the flames back to her hand and took a step forward. He watched, unable to move or talk. She raised her hand, but before she could deliver her final blow, an arrow flew within a hair's distance of her hand.

"That was a warning." Mirerien stepped out onto the street.

"You have no jurisdiction here," Maerishka complained. "This is none of your business, unless you are calling for an end to the treaty, for war between us." Her eyes flared with brief sparks of madness. Kern could almost believe she wanted war.

"I disagree."

"He is a citizen of Suriax, and therefore under my jurisdiction."

"He gave up his citizenship. As leader of Aleria, I hereby grant Kern Tygierrenon Alerian citizenship. As such, he is under our protection. You cannot touch him. Step back, or I will defend him with extreme prejudice." She punctuated her warning by pulling back another arrow to the ready. They stared at each other for several moments. Kern thought she would chance an attack when Pielere and Eirae stepped out of the shadows, swords drawn, standing on either side of their sister. Knowing she was outmatched, Maerishka lowered her hand.

CHAPTER EIGHT

THE SMELL OF BURNT FLESH AND BLOOD FILLED THE AIR. THE Tournament of Fire was always violent, but it finally lived up to its name. They would need to seriously consider new rules for the next tournament if they hoped to have any survivors … or participants. The wind shifted and smoke from a smoldering corpse blew in her face. They had to move the remainder of this year's tournament outside to accommodate the new abilities of the Suriaxian fighters. It became apparent after the third time the stadium tree caught fire that it would not be a suitable location for the fights. "Svanteese," Maerishka called. "Have the clerics work on fire protection spells to infuse with the tree before the next tournament. Also ask them about the feasibility for doing the same to the other buildings in town." With fires breaking out daily it was difficult for people to get any work done, although it was getting better. "Oh, and bring the Tournament Champion to me."

Maerishka went to her receiving chambers and removed her gloves, flexing her fingers in satisfaction. The clerics designed the gloves to allow her to touch others without accidentally killing them. She had a great deal more control now, but occasionally she got carried away and forgot herself. Even through the gloves others could feel her heat, but it was muted.

Svanteese led the champion, Zanden Fiereskai, into her chamber and left. Pouring herself a drink, she waited several moments before acknowledging him. Taking the time to finish her drink, she turned at last to face him. He stood, without a hint of impatience, still in the same spot Svanteese had left him. Still covered with blood and dirt from the final match, he was breathing hard, but he did not let any hint of his fatigue or any pain mar his stance. He stood at full attention, simply waiting for her to speak. "You did well today," she said at last.

"Thank you, Your Highness, but there were quite a few days I 'did well,'" he replied without a hint of conceit.

Walking up behind him, she placed a hand on his shoulder, waiting for his reaction. She was not disappointed. Under her fingers, his skin began to turn pink and blister. He did not flinch. She poured on the heat. Still, he did not move. Satisfied with his response, she removed her hand. Maerishka grinned. He was confident and not intimidated by her in the least. "Of all the contestants, you had the greatest mastery of your new abilities, though you refused to use them on any non-Suriaxian."

"I wanted to beat my opponents fairly. To use the fire on an opponent who couldn't use it back would have amounted to using a weapon against an unarmed man. That wouldn't have proven anything."

"Well, you certainly proved yourself. You showed an uncanny ability to read your enemy and judge how best to exploit his weaknesses within the first thirty seconds of every fight. Are you disappointed you didn't get to finish your match with Sardon?"

"He is a good opponent. I hope to get the opportunity to fight him again someday," he answered diplomatically.

"What would you say to working with him?"

"Your Highness?" The first hint of emotion entered his expression. His eyes were hopeful and confused.

"I find myself in need of someone with your particular skillset to train members of the Royal Guard and military. There are some who still find it difficult to master their fire abilities and could use extra guidance. I would also like you to develop new battle strategies to integrate these skills, particularly in group settings."

"You want our guys to be able to fight an enemy without burning all our own soldiers in the process."

"Precisely. I realize developing new fighting techniques is much easier if you have someone to work with. I would like you to work with Sardon for this purpose. Of course I would prefer it if you two could refrain from actually killing one another, but despite that restriction I imagine the sparing required for this task should prove enjoyable to the two of you."

Zanden grinned. "Yes, Your Highness."

"Good, I want weekly updates of your progress. You may go."

He bowed and left. Maerishka walked to her private chambers. She checked to see her bath was drawn and began to disrobe, dropping her gloves on top of the dress at her feet. She twirled her hair around and stuck a pin through it to keep it up at the back of her head. Stepping into the bath, she enjoyed the cool water the few seconds before it began to boil. Steam rose off the surface, filling the bathroom in seconds. She rested her head on the back of the tub and closed her eyes. It had been almost four months since she had seen her brother. So far he made good with his promise to leave her and Suriax alone, but she couldn't help thinking he could come back at any time and challenge her rule. Up until now she had the tournament to distract her, but that was over. She needed to focus on the future of Suriax.

"Oh, good, you're back." Alvexton came by the side of the

tub and bent down, kissing her passionately. Even that simple contact left his skin flushed. He took fire resistance potions daily just to be with her. He didn't seem to mind. Theirs was a mutually beneficial relationship. Once they married in a few months, she would quadruple her area of rule. Finally, her kingdom would rival Aleria's kingdom in size. And since he was human, she would only have to put up with him for fifty years, tops. As far as he was concerned he would get a wife who would always be young. Alvexton would also benefit from her military and Suriax's reputation. The southern plains were often plagued by raiders. Recently the attacks had grown worse, with whole villages wiped out with no explanation. Once Zanden created some viable battle strategies, she planned to send out a cinder unit to investigate. It would also give her people some good real world experience to test out his techniques and work out any problems. "I heard you were challenged again."

"That was hardly a challenge," she scoffed. "He was just some common street criminal who let a little power go to his head and thought he could actually take me on. It was barely worth the effort to kill him."

"Still, he is not the first. Such constant challenges are not good. As weak as they are in comparison to you, eventually one may catch you off guard. Besides, the uncertainty challenges generate could hurt your authority."

"What do you suggest?"

"I don't know. Make a law prohibiting them. Your people are all about laws."

She shook her head. "No, the people would never accept such a blanket declaration, but you may be on to something. I could design a law that structures the challenges, a list of criteria that must be met first." This could be the answer she needed. Kern had yet to make a move for her throne, but that could always change. Instituting a law to prohibit random challenges would not stop everyone, but it would help. "I knew I kept you around for some reason." She leaned out of the water and kissed him. Steam came off his face where her fingers touched it. "Care for a hot bath?"

Alvexton chuckled. "Darling, with you, that's the only kind there is."

"You win again." Kern cleared the game board and reset the pieces.

"Would you like to play another game?" Frex beamed excitedly.

"Sure." Kern smiled. His uncle looked fifty years younger. Whether it was spending time with his grand nieces and nephews, no longer having the stress of all his secrets resting on his soul or some strange side effect of being near Kern's siblings, he didn't know. Kern felt it too, to a certain degree. The longer he spent with them, the less he wanted to leave. For what it was worth, they seemed to like having him around. Mirerien invited him to spar with her a few times a week. She taught him to shoot a bow, and he taught her some of the subtler self-defense techniques he had learned in the Guard. Pielere spent time with him and Frex, just doing normal things. They fished, did some sightseeing, showing Kern around Aleria and taking Frex to places from his youth. Even Eirae was warming up to him. He gave Kern periodic updates from Suriax. Through interrogations and other information gathering Eirae knew a lot of the goings on, and he wasn't afraid to talk to Kern about it. It was through him they got updates on Marcy's brother, and for the past three months he snuck them an enchanted orb he used for spying so he, Marcy, Frex and Thomas could watch the tournament. He was the only one who didn't shy away from mentioning Suriax or expect them to forget where they came from.

They played a few more games, and then Frex got up to get more sweet rolls. Kern watched him talk to the baker, Elisteen, while her grandson Alnerand put bread in the oven. This was one of their frequent stops when they went on their walks with Pielere. Frex and Elisteen hit it off immediately sharing stories from Aleria's past. They talked often of King Emerien, how he was loved, how peaceful his reign was, and though Kern had never met his grandfather, he felt some pride at being related to such an incredible man. Knowing they would be awhile, he walked over to talk to Alnerand. The boy was also much happier than when they had met. Pielere put an end to their landlord's coercion. After a month of intense scrutiny and a substantial number of fines for ethics violations, Grieland sold his interests in his properties to a more honest landlord. All the residents signed fair lease agreements and were no longer forced into side jobs to keep their homes. With the money they received from Pielere, Elisteen was able to put in new oven and a storage room to keep her supplies at the back of the building. She could now reach her pans and materials without climbing on a ladder.

Kern made small talk, but his heart wasn't in it. Things were good, but he felt something was missing. He didn't have anything that drove him, a reason to exist. Elisteen and Alnerand had the bakery. He could see how much it meant to them both to be there, doing what they loved. His siblings had their work, and it meant everything to them. They made a real difference in people's lives. Marcy and Thomas felt some of his frustration and uncertainty. Their lives were just as jumbled as his, but they had their new relationship to distract them and make each day exciting. He had nothing and no one to call his own. Surrounded by family and friends, he felt alone.

The door opened, letting in a rush of cool air. In a couple of months it would be winter. "You aren't going to believe this." Eirae came in and dropped a letter in front of Kern. "You really got to her."

"Who?" Kern picked up the letter and read. "Suriaxian decree governing all challenges for the throne: Anyone wishing to take the throne of Suriax must travel to the Cliffs of Myremax to obtain one of the luminescent blood crystals found on the underside of the cliffs. Anyone bringing a blood crystal back to Suriax may challenge the current ruler to a dual of hand to hand combat. Fire is the only weapon allowed. The winner is to be determined by death or forfeit." The Cliffs of Myremax were home to several predatory animals. Although the crystals were beautiful and highly prized, getting them was a dangerous and often deadly task. The crystals got their name from the large quantity of blood spilled by thrill seekers and treasure hunters attempting to get one. Getting to the cliffs was also a long journey. Kern shook his head and put down the letter. "If she was really that worried about me, she could just have me killed in some 'accident.'"

"Word is there have been a lot of challenges in the past few months," Eirae confirmed, "but those were just minor annoyances, not any substantial threats as of yet. Make no mistake, this is about you. Stopping those other challenges is just a bonus."

"What about you guys? Are you worried about her acquiring so much territory with this marriage of hers? She could use it against you."

"We are of differing opinions, but she may be too busy with other issues to worry about us. Recent reports from the southern plains have been troubling. I think she might have gotten in over her head on this one. Of course, that is her problem. Have you considered the military appointment we offered you?"

"I don't think it's a good idea. I'm sure you can find someone better qualified in your own ranks."

"We would not have offered you the position unless we thought you could handle it."

He sipped on his mead. "I'm not really the leader type. Besides, if I were to accept, everyone would think it was nepotism, and any subordinates I had would be bitter about it. I know it would damage your credibility and cause a lot of unnecessary problems. It's not worth it."

Eirae didn't argue with any of his points. He accepted his own cup of mead and took a drink. "What will you do then?"

Kern couldn't think of an answer. Eirae finished his drink, put some money on the counter and motioned to the door. "Come with me."

After asking Frex to wait at the bakery, a request he was more than happy to comply with, they walked past the theater district to a small park. The focal point of the park was a stone fountain statue of a woman reading. Her eyes were on the book in her hand. Her other hand was by her head, entwined in her hair, flowing as though caught in the wind. The talent of the carver was unmistakable. Kern recognized the woman easily as his mother. The book was a perfect choice. He didn't remember much about her, but he remembered she loved to read. On every visit she would bring new books. When he was very young, she would read them to him. Eirae leaned against the railing surrounding the fountain and stared up at it. "We had the fountain put in just after her death." Kern looked at him in surprise. Clean, with sparkling, clear water around it, the statue looked brand new. "She died on this spot. There were once buildings here. There was a small bookstore she loved over on the corner. A riot broke out over a bad ruling from a judge. A man killed a robber in self-defense. The only problem was the judge was the brother of the dead man. When the defendant was sentenced to die, appeals were sent to our father. He could have overturned the ruling, but he had interests in another case that same judge was overseeing. He agreed to let the ruling stand if the judge ruled the way he wanted on that other case. The judge's home was a block from here. The day the man was executed, rioters burned the home to the ground with the judge inside. The riot spilled over this way. There was a bench here where she would sit and read. Someone recognized our mother and killed her as retribution for Veritan's actions. We had the fountain put in to remind us of the good times she had here and of the importance of our work." He turned to look at Kern. "Our destinies were forged on that day. No matter what we may disagree on, we know it is our responsibility to keep anything like that from happening here again. Everyone has something or someone they are responsible for in this life. You have to find out what that something is for you."

"How?"

"Once you find it, you'll know."

Kern gave a long glance back at the statue before following Eirae back to the bakery.

Lynnalin flipped through the many scrolls and tomes on her table and took notes. Suriax's magical awakening gave her new ideas for possible spell applications as of yet unexplored. Given the right combination of words and materials she could be onto some really useful spells. Already, the Cleric Guard was developing new fire protection spells to imbue in the homes and personal belongings of the citizens. She couldn't let the magi be outdone by a bunch of clerics. She was fourth decade after all. Most students stopped much earlier in their studies to go adventuring or took their basic magical knowledge and applied it to some practical profession in the city. There was a certain degree of arrogance involved as well. Semi-powerful magi began to feel there was nothing left to learn and resisted being taught. A good deal of the motivation came out of boredom. While sitting hunched over old scrolls and books could be enjoyable, it took someone with a tremendous amount of patience to keep it up for decades. Most people were drawn to magic for the excitement and the ability to blow people up and do flashy spells. Not that there was anything wrong with flashy spells, but sometimes a little subtly was required. Those who made it past the third decade understood that.

The doors to library opened. A page looked around anxiously, clearly uncomfortable to be there. He looked at every mage nervously. Most regarded him with a mixture of annoyance at being interrupted in their research and disinterest in his presence. His eyes settled on her. She felt the quill fall out of her hand. He walked briskly to her table, and stopped. "Lynnalin Moesaius?" She nodded. "You are hereby summoned by the Queen. Report immediately to the palace." He didn't wait for a response.

She sat in stunned silence for several seconds after the man left. Why would the Queen want to see her? Whatever the reason, it was not a good idea to keep her waiting. She stood and looked at the table. There was no time to put up everything. Grabbing her notes, she ran from the library. She caught up with the page as he exited the academy. They walked without speaking to the palace. She was shown to a lavishly decorated sitting room. Long, black velvet curtains hung from the windows. Strips of midnight blue fabric, trimmed in silver, were draped over and around the curtain rods. Candles lined every shelf and table. A fireplace raged across the room, making it uncomfortably warm. She contemplated sitting on one of the ornate sofas or chairs, but she was too anxious to sit. Walking over to the far wall, she busied herself looking at the many books displayed there. Some were history, of Suriax and the continent. There were a few fiction novels, mostly folklore related. The majority of the books were practical in nature. Topics ranged from architecture to botany to magic. A person could spend years, lifetimes learning all these subjects.

"So, you are the mage I've heard so much about."

Lynnalin jumped and saw Queen Maerishka standing in the open doorway. "You've heard of me?" Lynnalin asked in shock.

"Yes, my new head of military strategy, Zanden Fiereskai, recommended you. I need a mage to accompany a small team to investigate some activity in the southern plains. Have you ever ridden a marenpaie?"

"Not really," she answered honestly.

The queen nodded. Although the hounds were often used with the military or in long distance travel, few regular citizens had much practice riding them. "I currently have Zanden developing some new battle techniques. The team will leave in one month. Take that time to familiarize yourself with the hounds."

"Yes, Your Majesty."

"You may go."

Lynnalin rushed back to the academy. One month. There was much to do.

"You don't have to go."

"I do," Kern said, picking up his bag and slinging it over his shoulder. "I'm not cut out for palace life. I always wanted to travel, to see the continent. I think I'll finally do that."

Mirerien nodded and gave him a heartfelt hug. "We will miss you, brother. Please remember, you will always have a home here."

"Thank you."

"Here," Eirae handed Kern a dark blue cloak. It was well made and appeared very durable, but not fancy enough to draw unwanted attention on his travels. "We had it commissioned for you. It is laced with several spells that should help you on your journeys. While you wear it, should you require any healing, minor injuries will automatically begin to heal. Also, should it be lost or stolen, it will return to you on the following day."

"That's incredible." Kern couldn't believe the generosity of such a gift. He held the fabric delicately in his hands.

"We thought you could use something to keep warm, since you burned your other coats." Mirerien grinned.

Kern couldn't help grinning back. It was fitting that his jackets, symbols of his old life and service to Venerith, were now useless piles of ash and fabric. "You know, my jacket and shirt burned, but that scarf our mother made didn't burn."

"Mother used to put fire protection spells on all our clothing," Pielere explained. "It was one way she showed her displeasure at father's worship of Venerith. That in mind, we had a fire protection spell placed on this cloak as well."

"This is too much." Kern was overwhelmed. He was no stranger to magical items, but this was more than he ever though himself worthy of.

"That's not all." Pielere grinned. "If you put the hood up and whisper 'home,' it will teleport you here."

Kern didn't know what to say. Instead, he gave each of his brothers a warm handshake and gave Mirerien another hug. That just left one more thing to do. Going to his uncle's quarters, he smiled at the sight of children running around, playing and laughing. His uncle looked a hundred years younger now. Around his neck, he wore the scarf. Kern smiled. He almost hated to interrupt, but Frex caught sight of him and came over. "You are leaving, then?"

"Yes, for now. I'll be back often to visit. I just need to get out of here for a while and figure out where to go from here. But I want you to use that ring I gave you to call me if you need anything. I'll be back in a flash." He held up his cloak to accentuate his promise. They hugged warmly. Kern could see Frex was sad to see him go, but after hours of discussing it, he knew he understood and supported his decision.

"Where will you go?" Frex asked. It was the one thing they hadn't discussed, mainly because Kern didn't have an answer.

"Don't know, yet."

"Have you considered the mountains?" Thomas leaned against the doorway, his arm around Marcy. They smiled.

"That is where we are headed." Marcy looked lovingly up at Thomas.

Kern felt a reflexive stab of jealousy, but it was quickly gone as he looked at the happy faces of his two best friends. "Sure," he put his arms around them, leading them outside. "The mountains sound good."

ABOUT THE AUTHOR

"What do you want to be?"

When I was little, I answered that question with actor, writer, artist, astronaut, singer, fashion designer, and a few other things. Adults would grin at my answer and say I hadn't made up my mind, yet. I told them, "No, I want to be all of them."

I never understood the idea of limiting yourself to one thing. Life is so big. There is room for many adventures.

As I grew, I continued to draw. I wrote and performed songs at talent shows. I drew out designs for clothing and even sewed some outfits. I made my own wedding dress by hand. I studied digital design and learned to do some basic work in photo programs. Friends will tell you, I'm always jumping from one crazy project to another.

Again and again I've been told what I was doing was too difficult, I didn't know enough, I could never do it. And every time I've plunged head first into whatever my passion was driving me towards with a near unwavering faith that I could do anything I put my mind to. People always want to tell you what you can't do. We are all capable of incredible things when we have faith and believe in ourselves. You may not succeed at everything you do, but you will never succeed at something you do not try.

Despite my vast array of different interests, writing has long held a special place in my soul. When I was twelve years old, I spent an entire summer writing a story. Now, I often started projects without finishing them, before. This was different. I wrote every day. I wrote in the car, my room, and the laundromat. I wrote until, just as vacation was coming to an end, my story was done. I finished it. I knew in that moment, this was my calling in life. This was what I was meant to do.

From that moment on, I studied and wrote. Teachers and siblings told me to pursue a more practical career. I ignored them and followed my instincts.

When I needed a break, I still had all my other creative projects to help me recharge and have time to think. But I always returned to writing.

Through college, meeting and marrying my soulmate, working through jobs I hated, becoming mother to three wonderful boys, and homeschooling those same rambunctious boys, there have been challenges,. There were times I've had to take a break from regular writing to care for newborns and sick children. Though, even when I wasn't actively putting pen to paper, (yes, I still use good old fashioned notebooks and handwriting much of the time) my books are always somewhere in my mind. I've spent many nights crouched over paper, using the dim light from my phone or a night light to see enough to put down my thoughts, while my children sleep a few feet away. Writing is who I am.

My passion is in paranormal romances and fantasy books. I love writing about werewolves, and other shape shifters. I've also written about psychics.

I began writing fantasy after I was married. My husband and I used to get together with friends to play dungeons and dragons every Saturday. My husband wanted to create his own world with his own campaigns, so he enlisted my help in writing the background stories. He told me what his world was like and some of the key players and asked me to write backgrounds on other characters I told him what I had, and he added content or made changes to fit his vision. It was a lot of fun to work on this with him.

Later, I was looking for a quick project to write for nanowrimo (national novel writing month) and decided to put some of our notes into a full story of its own. That was the birth of our first collaborative fantasy book project. It is great to be able to share something that is such a big part of my soul with my husband. He has always supported my writing. Even when it hasn't paid off financially, he has never once asked me to stop.

I don't know what the future holds, but I know this is what I'm called to do.